SEA CUTTER

Book I
The Chronicles of
Nathaniel Childe

Tim Davis

ISBN:
9781502707109

*For Girls and Boys Everywhere
Who Still Long for Adventure
and Love to Read*

Thank you to my editor, Lisa Costantino, whose hard work and invaluable suggestions helped create this book.

Contents

CHAPTER ONE
Shipwreck

I kicked the plaque Mother had hung on the church wall.

Sacred
To the Memory
Of the Late
Captain Jonathan Childe
Of the Ship *Christopher*
Who in Battle with the Storm
Went Down with His Ship
August 3, 1769
This Tablet
Is Erected to his Memory
By His Son and His Widow

"He's not dead!" I yelled.

"Please, Nathaniel. It's been two years. He's not coming back," Mother begged.

"How can you give up on him?"

She put her hand on my shoulder, but I shook it off and ran from the church. When the world had said Father was dead, I'd defied it, but now Mother had given up hope.

"Whoa! Watch where you're going, lad."

A horse-drawn fish wagon rattled past on the cobblestones. The dying fish stared at me with wide, surprised eyes. A sob caught in my throat as I stumbled off the road, slamming into the church's elm tree like a man being dashed against the mast of his ship in a storm.

"Lost in a storm at sea," Wayland, my father's first mate, had said. He was my father's best friend—my best friend too.

"He stayed on his ship to the end," he'd told me. "He was cutting through the lines tangled around the last lifeboat. He wanted to save James Talbot and Robert Long."

"But you didn't see him go under?" I'd pleaded.

"A towering wave broke over the ship. 'Twas so big it snapped the mast off with a great crack, and it swept all three off the deck. The ship sank fast, the lifeboat still tangled. I'm sorry, Nat. Remember your father acted nobly staying on his ship to save the last of his crew."

Mother found me sitting under the gnarled old elm. I wouldn't look at her. She sat down beside me anyway and stroked my hair while humming a song we all used to sing together. Sometimes when I was the angriest with Mother was when I needed her the most. I turned and cradled my head against her heart, clinging to her as she rocked me gently.

"Let's go home," she said after a while. "I need your help."

"With what?" We walked along the cobblestone road.

"A problem many eleven-year-old boys might not understand, but you're smarter than most boys, and we have to be smart together to keep our home. We're almost out of money."

"But the trading company owes us thousands of pounds."

"They've figured out a way not to pay it."

A bomb went off in my head. "We'll make them pay!"

Three red-coated British soldiers glanced over in surprise and laughed.

Mother lowered her head. "We'll have to make our

own money."

We were passing the docks. The masts of great whaling and merchant ships towered above us, while the smell of salt and tar filled my nostrils. Greedy seagulls soared everywhere, filling the air with their harsh "caw-caw-caw."

"I could go to sea. I'm old enough to work as a cabin boy."

She swayed and sank on her knees.

"Mother! What's the matter?" I held her shoulders so she wouldn't fall to the ground.

She took my hand in both of hers. "Nathaniel, promise me you'll never go to sea."

"But I want to be a ship's captain, like Father."

"I've lost too much to the sea." Her face was deadly pale. "Promise me. Promise me, Nat."

"I promise," I said, stunned by her fervor.

"Promise me. Promise!" she whispered again.

"I promise, Mother. I promise. I promise."

Mother took a deep breath and stood. "Nat, do you know what Father would say if he were here?" We walked on. "He'd say, 'Son, this is no time to be talking of going to sea. Mother needs a man around the house. Stick by her, Nat. Take care of her. Make me proud of you.'"

I nodded, puffing out my chest and walking taller

as we passed a chandlery overflowing with ship's tackle waiting to be repaired. I stopped, staring at the pile.

"I know. We'll open a chandlery in our home, like Grandfather. He taught me to use the furnace and the anvil and—and all sorts of things."

She cocked her head, studying the mound of broken tackle. "And I grew up with it. It's hard work, though."

"I'm big and strong for my age, and good with my hands."

"You are. Do you think you could do it?"

We reached our heavy, red-painted door. Ambition swelled my heart.

"Mother, you can count on me. I'm going to make sure you have everything you need. Everything you would've had if…. Everything you would've had if Father were still here."

* * *

We opened the chandlery, hired a bellows boy, and I threw myself into the work. Mother kept the books and sold supplies. By twelve, I was doing as much work as a grown man.

Yet even though we worked hard, we weren't making money.

One night, I studied the account books and found

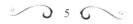

out why. Many of our customers had cheated
Mother. I couldn't believe it. Cheating a poor widow.

*I guess I should've learned from the trading
company.* My lip curled into a sneer.

Chief among the cheaters was Captain Crawford,
who, by my reckoning, had swindled us out of seventy-
six pounds.

Our house shook the next morning as his huge hand
slammed the door when he came to collect his
astrolabe, which I'd stayed awake repairing until the
sun rose.

"Ah!" he exclaimed, starting to pick it up. "Looks
better than new."

I grabbed the astrolabe too.

"Don't pull," I warned. "It will ruin the repair. You
can have it when you pay the seventy-six pounds you
tricked us out of."

Crawford turned red and bristled. "I'm used to
dealing with your mother about payment."

"You'll be dealing with me from now on, and it's
going to be cash on the barrelhead."

"You're a mere—"

"Seventy-six pounds, or no astrolabe."

Crawford growled a curse but pulled out his purse
and paid.

"See if I ever come back here," he snapped, before

slamming the door even harder.

But he did come back in three days when his chronometer stopped working and he needed it repaired at once.

So it went with our other customers. I became known as a nasty person to deal with, but the sailors brought me their broken tackle anyway because I did a superb job. Our chandlery prospered, but Mother wasn't happy with my tough attitude.

"Nat, can't we run the chandlery without being so hard on people all the time?"

"Sure, we could just let everybody walk all over us." I pounded out a twist in a whaling harpoon. "Have you forgotten what the trading company did to us? Have you forgotten how our customers cheated us? That's what the world is like. If you're soft, they'll take everything you have."

"But I'm worried about you. People in town say you're mean."

"Let them say what they want! No one gave us a hand when Father died. To blazes with what they think."

"Wayland's been helping us," Mother faltered.

Wayland, at sea for the last two years, sent us money whenever he could.

"He's different," I mumbled.

"Nat, for the peace of your own soul—"

I threw down my hammer. "You think I run the shop wrong? Fine. I'll hire out on a ship and get out of your way."

Mother paled. "No, Nat. You promised." She clutched my hand, but I yanked it away.

"I am. I'm going to the docks right now to sign on." I stalked out of the room.

"Nat! Don't!"

I slammed the door.

I didn't intend on going to sea, for I was still determined to protect Mother, but it hurt when she found fault. I lashed out, stopping her censure however I could. Instead of going to the docks, I crept below the window and listened to her cry.

"Dear Lord, don't let Nat go to sea," she prayed between sobs. "When it seemed we couldn't have a child, you brought him to us. Please don't take him away from me."

I crept away, feeling guilty about making her cry. I wondered what she meant about not being able to have a child, but since I'd heard it while eavesdropping, I couldn't ask her.

After that, Mother let me do things my own way.

Two months later, a letter arrived from Maine. Aunt Mary, Mother's sister, was quite sick. Uncle

William asked if Mother could come help nurse her.

Mother wanted to go, and she planned to close the chandlery for a while. I argued that we'd lose steady customers if we closed, and I persuaded her to let me stay behind and run the chandlery myself.

"That way you can stay as long as Aunt Mary needs you. If I stay here, I can even send you money for medicines. Go help Aunt Mary. I'll be fine."

Nothing could equal the satisfaction of the grateful hug she gave me the day she left. I'd succeeded in becoming the one she could count on.

Her rattling coach rolled away while she cried and waved to me as if she'd never see me again. I thought it better to act manly, so I waved a few times and then strolled away with my hands in my pockets even before the coach was out of sight.

If I'd known the peril that awaited me, I never would've said farewell so casually.

CHAPTER TWO
The Sea Chest

Living by myself was lonelier than I'd expected.

The nights hit me hardest. I tossed and turned through nightmares about Father. He clung to a beam while the sea washed him to an unknown island. He called, "Nat! Nat! Nat!" while Mother and I stood at his plaque, saying, "He's dead. He's dead. He's dead."

"No! He's not!" I woke at my own voice.

I struggled through work at the chandlery. Customers came, but they weren't friendly, since I hadn't been running the chandlery in a friendly way.

Sundays I didn't go to church. Let Captain Crawford and the other cheaters sing their Psalms. I hated standing near them while they pretended to be so pious, and it confused me to hear the pastor talk about God's goodness with Father's death plaque hanging on the wall.

One Sunday night, I determined to stay awake to avoid the nightmares. I was sitting at the table, staring at the yellow flame of a candle, when I heard a horse and wagon clatter to our door and the *thunk* of something heavy hitting the ground.

A knock, and a cheerful voice bellowed, "Anybody home?"

I threw open the door. "Wayland!"

He gathered me in a bear hug, his bushy gray beard tickling my face as he gave me a laughing kiss on the top of my head. His twinkling blue eyes looked me up and down, every line of his face molded in a smile.

"You've grown up, young man."

"I'm thirteen now," I answered, grinning like I was still eleven.

"So you are. So you are. Now, lad, where's your mother? It's a wonder she can sleep through all this ruckus."

"She's in Maine nursing her sister."

He scratched the side of his great hooked nose. "Now what'll I do?" I heard him mutter.

"Are you here to stay for a while?" I asked, a plea in my voice.

"The ship I was on, the *Southern Lady*, sails

tomorrow, but I've signed off."

"Oh! Great!"

His brow furrowed. "Nat, I brought something with me. I planned to show it to your mother before I showed it to you, because…because I thought it might wake painful memories for you."

"What is it?"

"'Tis your father's sea chest, addressed to your mother and you."

My stomach tightened. "How's that possible?"

"It was sent before the shipwreck. Then somehow it got lost over these past four years."

"From Father…." I faltered.

"Nat. Are you going to be all right?" He clutched my shoulder, searching my eyes.

I nodded. "Let's get it."

It took both of us to drag the sea chest into the house because it wasn't made of wood, but steel. Father had always kept it polished, but now rust pitted the surface. On the top was a brass plaque that read:

To Be Delivered to
Jennifer and Nathaniel Childe of New Bedford
Sent by Captain Jonathan Childe
Of the Good Ship *Christopher*
In care of Captain Peter Croop

Of the Good Ship *Majesty*
On this 26th Day of June
In the Year of Our Lord 1769

Father had always sent us sea chests full of gifts, although he'd never sent his own steel trunk before. They contained exotic fabrics for my mother to sew into dresses, foreign toys and curiosities for me, and always a long letter about his voyages.

We enjoyed the letters best. We'd read them over and over by the fire until his ship put into port again.

How merry we were when word came that the *Christopher* was putting into port! We'd run to the docks. As soon as Father saw Mother he'd sweep her off her feet with a big hug and kiss, and then hoist me onto his shoulders and we'd talk and laugh all the way home....

I noticed Wayland's anxious gaze.

I spoke as evenly as I could. "I've heard of the *Majesty*. Didn't she go down about the same time as Father's ship?"

"Yes. 'Twas due in Boston in April, but she sank in the same storm that took the *Christopher*. The sea chest must not have been on board."

"Where did you find it?"

"On the *Southern Lady*. 'Twas quite odd. We found

it on the deck one morning. No one knew where it
came from. I told the captain I knew you and offered to
bring it to you."

"Look at these scratches around the lock.
Somebody's tried to break into it."

"Which makes me wonder if the trunk wasn't lost at
all, but stolen."

A burning rage ignited. "Who would do that?"

"I don't know, but he must've mashed his best tools
trying to break into it."

We both knew the strength of the steel.

"I'll get the key."

I ran to Mother's room and grabbed the key from her
jewelry box. We threw back the lid and stared in shock.

"Rags." I said, my stomach falling. "Why would he
send us rags?"

"Maybe he packed something else further down."

I plunged my hands through the rags and felt
something hard. I pulled out a knife in a sheath, the hilt
elaborately decorated. I drew the blade to reveal two
sharp edges.

"It's a dagger," I said.

"Looks like a small sword."

"It does." I swung the dagger around in the air,
pretending to be a knight from the old stories.

"Be careful with that," Wayland warned, backing

away. "It looks sharp enough to cut through steel."

"Really?" I swung the dagger down on the steel chest.

"Nat!" We both dove out of the way as the dagger bounced high into the air, then plunged with a deadly *thunk* into the wooden floor.

"I'm sorry," I mumbled, hanging my head. "Did I ruin the dagger?"

He pulled it from the floor. "I don't see a scratch, but look at the chest."

A knick scarred the steel.

Reverently, he returned the dagger to me. "This is a lethal weapon."

"I'll be more cautious with it," I vowed, sheathing and carefully laying it on the table. "What else is in here?"

I dug into the chest again and pulled out a red leather box about as big as Wayland's fist. Father had written on the top, "For My Dearest Wife."

I looked at the keyhole and knew exactly where the key lay—in a locket Mother wore around her neck.

"We can break this box open with my dagger."

Wayland put his hand over the box, shaking his head. "This box is for your mother."

"But—"

He looked me in the eye with a sternness I knew

wouldn't waver.

"You're right." I gulped. "Let's look for more."

We pulled out rags and found a package bound in oiled skin with "For Nathaniel" inked on it. I unwrapped the oilskin. It was an old copy of Benjamin Franklin's *Poor Richard's Almanac*.

"Why'd he send me this?"

He scratched his head. "'Tis a good almanac."

"That still doesn't make sense."

"See if there's anything inside it."

I opened the almanac and a folded paper fluttered out of the leaves, falling to the floor.

"A letter. A letter to Mother and me."

I opened the sheet with shaking hands, but the letter wasn't what I'd expected. Nor did I have any idea about the strange and dangerous adventure it would start.

CHAPTER THREE
The Map

Dearest Jennie,

I am sorry this letter is so brief, but I write in haste before the *Majesty* sails. I have decided to make a voyage for great treasure. I'll explain it all to you when I return, but in the meantime, keep this trip a secret.

If I don't return, tell Nathaniel to play the game that used to make me laugh so hard. He will find a message. All of my love to you and my brave son.

Love, Jonathan

"Father says that if he doesn't return, I should play a game to find a message."

"What game?"

"How should I know? We played a hundred games. Maybe we'll find a clue if we finish with the chest."

We pulled out every rag but found nothing else. I kicked the trunk.

Wayland looked at me keenly. "They say walking helps you think. Would you care to come take a midnight look at the *Sea Cutter*?"

I brightened, for I loved going aboard Wayland's sloop. He'd bought the sailboat as an old wreck, but he'd repaired it over the years so now everything shone better than new. She cut through the waves like a knife, and that's why he called her the *Sea Cutter*.

"What shall we do with these gifts and letter?" I asked.

"Let's keep them safe with us."

We lit a lantern and I bolted the iron lock on our door. Our boots made a loud *clip-clop* on the empty cobblestone streets, while our lantern threw only a faint glow.

Out of the corner of my eye I thought I saw something move in the shadows. I clutched Wayland's arm. "What was that?"

He stopped, searching the shadows. "I don't see anything."

We kept a good watch the rest of the way but saw

nothing. Soon we reached the *Sea Cutter*'s slip. The lantern shone on the mellow honey color of the polished oak deck and gleamed against the whiteness of the glossy hull. Her single mast towered toward the glowing stars.

We unlocked the hatch, climbed down the companionway, and lit a lantern hanging from the ceiling. It showed a captain's quarters with a desk for calculating navigation and a hammock.

We went through a door into the galley where Wayland had cooked me many a fine meal, then went further forward into a small cabin in the bow where the crew berthed. He lifted a hatch in the floor between the two hammocks and peered into the hold where he stored the sails.

He sniffed.

"It smells as if the sails stayed dry."

A hatch in the roof of the crew's cabin gave a man a way to lift himself quickly to the deck. He opened it to let in the cool night air.

"How about a cup of coffee?" he asked as he went back into the galley and lit his kerosene stove. He took a bag of coffee beans from the shelf, ground them, and brewed us a pot of strong coffee. Then we sipped it from steaming cups while Wayland searched through the almanac.

"Here's something," he said.

"Let me see." I leaped to his side.

He pointed at one of the little sayings Franklin liked to put in his almanac: "All work and no play makes Jack a dull boy."

A strong underline ran beneath, with two strokes under the word "play."

"There it is again. 'Play.' But how in the world am I supposed to know what game to play?"

Wayland dragged his hand down his face in thought, drawing his mouth into a deep frown.

I burst out laughing.

"What? What'd I do?"

"For a moment you looked like Old Bill Hicker."

"Old Bill Hicker." He chuckled. "I saw him today, still pushing his cart selling limes. Looks as grouchy as ever."

"His face is so sour it looks like he sucks on his own limes. All puckered, like this." I scrunched my face and he laughed. "When we'd buy limes from him, I'd always take a suck on one and then walk around the house with my face puckered, pretending to push a wagon. It made Father laugh 'til he was gasping for breath."

"Sounds fun."

"We'd play a game with the lime juice, pretending

we were spies writing secret messages. When the juice dried, I couldn't see the message until I heated the paper over a candle…."

I stopped short. Wayland and I stared at each other.

"That's it! Invisible ink. Where would he have written the message?"

"What about on the letter?"

"Light a candle."

I held the letter over the flame, moving it to warm the whole paper. Nothing happened.

"Maybe it's got to be warmer." I held the letter closer to the candle, and it flared into flame.

"Stop!" I waved it in the air, but in seconds the letter was flaky gray ash drifting through the cabin.

"The last letter from Father!"

"I'm sorry, Nat."

I swallowed. "But that doesn't mean the message isn't somewhere else."

"No, it doesn't." Wayland patted my shoulder. "Where do you want to look next?"

"How about the blank cover page at the beginning of the almanac?"

"Fine," he answered, with a twinkle in his eyes. "Just let me fetch some water in case you set that page on fire too."

"You'd better get a bucket, in case I set the whole

almanac on fire," I kidded back, holding the page a safe distance from the flame.

We both gasped as a map appeared.

"That's not lime juice," I breathed. "It's red."

The map showed a large island with longitude and latitude numbers written alongside. Pictures of reefs and wrecks surrounded the island with arrows snaking through them. Father had written, "Hidden reefs. Follow arrows for safe passage to Perlas Grandes."

"Perlas Grandes!" Wayland held his fist to his mouth, frowning.

"An island with huge pearls?"

"Everyone says it's only a legend, Nat," he warned.

I stared at the map. Then a cannon went off in my chest.

"Wayland. The longitude and latitude. Isn't that near where Father's ship went down?"

"It is."

"Then Father might be on that island!"

"Nat, I know how you must feel, but look at my own map."

He unrolled a perfect map of the South Atlantic and pointed at the spot where Father had positioned Perlas Grandes. "There's nothing there, Nat. The only islands anywhere nearby are St. Helena and Tristan da Cunha. Hundreds of ships have sailed these waters and seen nothing."

"If a ship did see it, the hidden reefs would explain why it never came back to tell about it." I formed a plan.

Wayland looked me right in the eyes. "What are you thinking of doing?"

"What do you mean?"

He slapped his knee and chuckled. "Oh, Nat. Don't you think I've known you long enough to read your face? Now come on. You're planning something."

I averted my eyes. "I guess I'm thinking of hiring onto a ship as a cabin boy, and then convincing the captain to search that area."

"Why, you're a green swab if you think a captain would listen to a cabin boy. He'd hang you on the spot for impertinence."

"I'd think of something," I protested.

"What about your mother? She told me that you promised her never to go to sea."

"When I came back with Father, she'd have to understand."

"If you came back, you mean."

I bristled. "You can't stop me."

Wayland looked intently at me, then stood to make some more coffee. "No. I don't suppose I could stop you. When you plan to do something, you don't let anything stop you. Here's a better idea. Why don't you and I sail the *Sea Cutter* out to search for Perlas Grandes?"

"Do you mean it?"

"I could keep you safer than you'd be with your own plan. We can sail exactly where we want. Search as long as we want."

Something broke in me, and I sobbed. Wayland sat beside me, rubbing my back.

"How can I ever thank you?" I dried my eyes.

"By making two promises."

"What promises?"

"Promise you'll write to your mother and get permission to sail with me, and promise that if she doesn't give her permission, you won't try to go some other way."

"But she'll have to agree when she learns about what we've found!"

"I need her permission. Otherwise she might think I'm trying to take you back…." He stopped, flustered.

"Take me back where?"

"Back…uh…back to a life on the sea." He coughed, looking away.

I was confused. I'd never been on the sea.

He turned back toward me, his eyes like nails. "Promise me, Nat. Promise you won't go to sea without your mother's permission."

"I—I promise."

"Put your hand on my Bible. Promise again. Word for word."

I put my hand on his Bible. "I promise I'll get Mother's permission, and if she doesn't agree, I won't go to sea."

He smiled and put his arm around my shoulders. "If Perlas Grandes is out there, we'll find it. If your father is on the island, we'll find him too. Now, come on, I'll take you home. Write to your mother in the morning, then meet me here. I've got to start teaching you how to sail this old boat."

I was too excited to sleep when Wayland left me at my door. The house seemed hot and stuffy after the brisk night walk, so I opened the window.

I took out Father's gifts and laid them in a row—the dagger, *Poor Richard's Almanac*, and the mysterious box. I shook it but heard nothing.

I opened the almanac to the map of Perlas Grandes and then rolled out one of Father's maps of the South Atlantic to daydream of the oceans we'd soon sail.

My head started nodding. I took the dagger, the almanac, and the red box into my bedroom, leaving Father's map on the table. In bed, my daydreams turned to the dreams of sleep—the first happy dreams

I'd had in years.

It was still deepest night when a faint sound woke me. Through the space at the bottom of my door, I saw shifting light.

CHAPTER FOUR
Snake

I grabbed my dagger and crept out of bed, but a board creaked. Instantly, the light went out and I heard someone scrambling. I threw open the door and saw a dark form slithering out the window.

I sprang toward it but in the dark knocked my knee hard against a heavy wooden rocker and fell down. By the time I got to the window, I couldn't see anybody on the street.

"Coward!" I shouted into the night. With trembling hands, I slammed the glass shut, then limped to the table and lit the lantern.

The map of the South Atlantic was gone.

I took the lantern off its peg and searched through the room. Nothing else was missing. I rubbed my knee. It was starting to swell and hurt worse. None of this made any sense. Why would a thief break into our house, only to steal a map of the South Atlantic?It was the deepest, deadest part of night, but I was far too shaken to sleep, so I limped up and down the room.

"Wayland will teach me how to sail the *Sea Cutter* today," I said, trying to cheer myself, but instead my body tightened.

"The letter to Mother!" I remembered with a lurch in my stomach. Last night I'd been sure she'd give me permission to sail with Wayland. How could I have been so dumb? She'd never agree.

An ugly thought wormed its way into my head. "Wayland tricked me. He knew all the time Mother would never give permission."

The night looked even blacker. Cruel faces seemed to be floating in the dark corners of the room.

"But what's more important, keeping a promise or finding Father? If Wayland won't take me on the *Sea Cutter*, I'll find another way to go."

I fell into an impossible daydream of having enough money to hire my own ship to sail out to Perlas Grandes. Then the image of the red box flashed into my mind. I jumped up, certain of what it contained.

I placed it on the table, poising my dagger carefully above it, and gave the box a light tap.

It sprang open, revealing a large, white, glowing sphere nestled in the blood-red velvet.

I grabbed it. A pearl from Perlas Grandes.

*   *   *

I limped onto the docks when the sun rose, admiring the massive hulls and tall masts of the trading ships with a zealous eye. Before the day was over, I'd hire one of these ships to rescue Father. The pearl nestled in my pocket and I'd already written a letter to Mother.

> Dear Mother,
>
> Wayland brought home Father's sea chest addressed to us. Someone stole it four years ago. Father drew a secret map for me of an island in the South Atlantic called Perlas Grandes. I believe Father is marooned there, and I'm going to sail there to rescue him.
>
> He also sent a giant pearl, big enough for me to hire a ship. Try not to worry. Only think how happy we'll be when I bring Father back!
>
> Love, Nat

I'd posted the letter on my way to the docks, beyond which a cloud bank massed along the eastern horizon and dimmed the sun. The waves looked as dull as lead.

The docks swarmed with men: ship owners in satin frock coats, tough-looking sailors covered with tattoos, and expert whalers with their favorite harpoons slung over their shoulders.

Some sailors swapped stories over their long clay pipes and talked about newly discovered trade routes. Others scrambled up masts, dangled from the rigging, and even dived into the water to clean the submerged hulls. Their shouts, commands, and coarse laughter competed with the screaming gulls.

A ship's captain with a black beard strolled over to me.

"You looking to go out to sea, sonny?" he asked. "I'm looking for a new cabin boy."

"I want to go to sea, but not as a cabin boy."

He laughed. "A cabin boy is generally how a young lad starts out. Or do you be hankering to start out as the first mate?"

I tried to laugh with him, for I'd said too much too soon. "Tell me. Where are you bound?"

"We run regular routes 'tween various ports and Cape Town on the southern tip of Africa."

My excitement grew. "Then you must know the South Atlantic well."

"Know it?" He slapped his hand over his eyes. "I could sail it with my eyes closed."

"Have you ever seen any islands out there?"

"Sure. St. Helena and Tristan da Cunha. We stop there all the time if it's them you be hankering to see."

"But there's supposed to be another island in the South Atlantic—Perlas Grandes."

He threw back his head with a bellowing laugh.

A smelly, slim, oily-looking fellow sauntered over. A tattoo of a snake coiled around his arm, ending with the open mouth and poisonous fangs of a viper. Its red, vicious eyes stared right at me.

"What's the joke, Captain?" the oily man asked while looking at me with a cruel grin.

"This lad wants us to sail the *Southern Lady* to Perlas Grandes!"

Southern Lady. The ship Wayland had sailed aboard.

The smelly man put a hand on my shoulder, the tattoo of the snake reaching for my neck. "We'll take you to Perlas Grandes, little one." His grin grew even crueler. "But first we got to make stops at Fairy Land and the Island Above the Clouds. Ain't you afraid of the Great Sea Serpent? He don't like people sailing to Perlas Grandes."

They both erupted into laughter again, while a few other sailors ambled over.

"We got us a new cabin boy?" one of them asked.

"Oh, yes," said the tattooed man. "One who can

amuse us with fairy tales. He wants to sail to Perlas Grandes."

I shrugged the hand off my shoulder. I was furious at him. I hated him.

"How do you know it's not out there? New islands are always being discovered."

The oily man snickered. "Maybe in the Pacific, sonny, but not in the Atlantic. Better go back and study your maps."

My voice rose. "I dare say I know the maps as well as you do. My father traced out every voyage he made on our maps."

"If your father used maps with Perlas Grandes on them, I'll bet the captain never asked him to help navigate. Kept him locked in the loony bin, no doubt."

"My father *was* the captain," I said, with a threat in my voice.

"Was? What happened? Lost his ship?"

"Take it easy on the lad, Snake," one of the sailors spoke up. "I recognize this boy now. He's the son of Captain Jonathan Childe of the *Christopher*. A finer captain you'd never meet."

"The *Christopher*?" the captain mused. "Didn't the *Christopher* go down in the South Atlantic about four years ago?"

"Yes," the oily man said. "Probably went down

searching for Perlas Grandes."

"And what if he was?" I shouted, trembling with rage.

"I've sailed the Atlantic all my life. I'll name myself a fool if I ever see one bit of evidence Perlas Grandes exists."

"Then that's just what you are—a fool!"

I pulled out the pearl, which glowed with flawless beauty. Every man gasped in astonishment. Every man except the oily one. While the others stared in awe at the pearl, he looked me in the eye with a triumphant gleam.

"I thought so," he mouthed so only I could see, and a killing look shot from his eyes.

I stood frozen a moment, then ran wildly.

I dodged through the alleys of New Bedford. Get away from Snake. Get away from those eyes. Get home and bar the door. Grab my dagger. Defend myself.

I reached my door, my lungs on fire, my knee screaming pain. I threw open the lock, dashed in, and barred the door.

"You have something I want," a voice hissed behind me, making me jump.

Snake gloated at me, holding my dagger.

I lunged toward the window, but something hit me

hard on the back of my head.

Sparks flew from my eyes as I hurtled into darkness.

CHAPTER FIVE
The Lie

My eyes blurred open. Wayland, on his knees beside me, held my head. I groaned. My skull felt like a volcano.

"Ah. There you are, lad. There you are. Just take it easy."

"What happened?"

"You were robbed." Clothes, maps, tools lay scattered on the floor. "Did you see the thief?"

"Tattoo of a snake." Memory drifted back like thin wisps of smoke.

"Snake! From the *Southern Lady*." He spotted the empty red leather box. "He took the pearl."

My hand darted to my pocket. No pearl. "Get to the

Southern Lady before she sails!" I struggled to my feet.

"She's already sailed. Did he get the almanac?"

I stumbled into my bedroom, clutching my throbbing head with one hand and my aching knee with the other. Snake had thrown everything around, but I spied the almanac in a corner.

"It's still here."

"Thank goodness." Wayland smiled with relief. "Then we can still sail."

"Wait. How'd you know the box contained a pearl?"

He sighed. "All right. I'll tell you everything. Your father showed me the pearl to convince me to search for Perlas Grandes."

"So it exists! Why didn't you tell me last night?"

"Because I still don't think it exists, and I didn't want to get your hopes too high."

"But the pearl—"

"Could be from anywhere. The map of Perlas Grandes I considered a forgery."

"Why'd you agree then?"

"Friendship, and it was his ship. He knew I didn't believe but would help him search."

"Why didn't you tell us?"

"Because I knew you'd want to search for it too, and the map went down with the ship. I didn't know your father had sent you a copy. When I saw that, I decided to sail you out there, but only with your mother's permission. Did you write to her?"

How could I have distrusted Wayland?

"Yes, I wrote to her." I studied a nail in the floor.

"Good. I wrote to her too."

"Why'd you do that?" I clutched his sleeve.

"I thought it would help convince her to let you sail with me."

Now Mother would get two letters at the same time —mine telling her about the pearl and hiring a ship, and Wayland's asking her permission to take me on the *Sea Cutter*.

She'd write to Wayland telling him she didn't want me to go to sea, and about my plan. We wouldn't sail, and he would know I'd broken my promises.

I knew I should admit what I'd done, but the words stuck in my throat. If only I hadn't posted…. Wait. It might not have gone yet.

I sprang to the door. "I've got an errand to run. I'll meet you at the *Sea Cutter*."

I left Wayland scratching his head.

"Mr. Barton," I panted as I threw open the post office's door. "I slid a letter to my mother under your door this morning, and I—"

"My goodness, Nat, what happened to your head?" Mr. Barton boomed out as cheerfully as if I were bringing him a cherry pie.

"It's nothing. I need—"

"And you're limping too. You're knee, is it?"

"I—"

"Wait." He put forward his chubby hands. "Give me three guesses how it happened." He put both hands on his gleaming bald scalp, closed his eyes, and furrowed his brow. "Guess one: you sneezed so hard your knee flew up and hit your head."

"Mr. Barton, the letter—"

"Guess two: you got out of bed in the wrong direction and were walking around on your head until you cracked your knee into the door."

"Mr. Barton, I'm in a—"

"Guess three: your favorite little lady thrashed you."

"I don't have a…" I started to say, turning red. "Mr. Barton, I need that letter back."

"Why didn't you say so, lad?" He looked as jovial as if he'd found a pot of money. "Precious minutes are being wasted. Ned has it. He was saddling when I left him."

I dashed outside to see Ned galloping away in the distance.

"Why, it looks like he just rode," Mr. Barton said, coming behind me. "He must've left while we were talking."

I had a wild impulse to beat Mr. Barton on his shiny bald head for blathering away while Ned left.

"How long will it take Ned to deliver my letter?"

"I'd say about five or six days. You should hear back from her within two weeks."

Two weeks at the most before Wayland received Mother's response. I hobbled down to the pier.

"Ah, there's my sailor." Wayland grinned. "Ready to go?"

"Yes, but…."

"But what?" He cocked his head.

"Nothing," I muttered.

For the rest of the day he taught me about the *Sea Cutter*. While he spliced a stranded white line, I asked, "What if Mother says I can't sail with you? Would you try to talk her into it?"

"Absolutely not," he said, still intent on his line. "Even if I were halfway across the sea, I'd turn around and come right back. I've written to her in favor of sailing, and now what your mother says goes."

Over the next week and a half, Wayland taught me to sail the *Sea Cutter*, even taking us out of the harbor into the sea. These should've been among the best days of my life, but I knew soon Wayland would get a letter from Mother that would ruin everything.

I hardly ate or slept the night before the eleventh day.

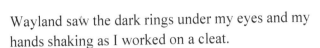

Wayland saw the dark rings under my eyes and my hands shaking as I worked on a cleat.

"What's wrong, Nat? You look sick. Perhaps you should be in bed."

"I'm fine. Just excited about the journey."

Although I dreaded the letter, I didn't want to be away when it arrived. I winced whenever I heard a shout, for I thought it was Mr. Barton booming his way down to deliver it to Wayland.

But no letter came, nor on the next day or the day after. That meant it would almost certainly arrive tomorrow.

That night, I sat staring at a shadowy corner when a plan stunned me. I'd write a letter myself, but I'd make it look like it came from Mother! We'd sail before the real letter arrived.

I dashed to Mother's room and pulled out a package of her love letters to Father. In the deep of the night, I mastered Mother's hand well enough to write the letter.

In the morning, I ran to the docks.

"Wayland! Wayland! Mother's letter arrived. It says we can go!"

Wayland grinned and took the letter from my hand. His grin turned into a confused frown as he read it out loud:

Dear Nat,

I am so glad to hear about your plans to sail with Wayland and look for Father. It is a good plan, so leave as soon as you can. Tell Wayland I'm sorry I don't have time to answer his letter too, but Mary is so sick that I am very busy. I understand all the dangers perfectly, but I am sure you will be fine as long as you are with Wayland. Good luck!

Love, Mother

"What's wrong?" My hair tingled as I watched his face.

"'Tis—'tis just not the kind of letter I would have expected your mother to write. But 'tis your mother's hand, all right."

I looked at my shuffling feet. "She said she was pretty busy with Aunt Mary."

"Aye. That must be it." Wayland's grin returned. "Well, my lad, it looks as if we're off to the open sea."

"Hooray! I'll get my sea bag and we'll be right off."

I dashed home and wrote a second letter to Mother.

Dearest Mother,

Things did not go as I had planned. I lost the pearl, and now I have had no choice but to

trick Wayland into thinking it's all right with you if he sails me out to rescue Father. It's not Wayland's fault. Don't blame him. I know you're going to be worried, Mother. But it's worth everything to find Father. Don't you think so? Please try to think about that.

Your Loving Son, Nat

I grabbed my sea bag, hung a "Closed" sign on our chandlery, and headed to Mr. Barton's.

"Ah, Nat, well met," he boomed when I opened his door. "I've just received a letter from your mother for Wayland, and I'm on my way down to the *Sea Cutter* to give it to him."

CHAPTER SIX
The Unexpected Visitor

Ice froze my spine. "A letter from my mother to Wayland?"

"I'm going right down to the *Sea Cutter* to find him," Mr. Barton declared.

"Wait!" I held my hands in front of me. "Give me three guesses why Ned was late. Guess one. He got hungry along the way and ate his horse."

He roared with laughter. "Good guess. Two more."

"Guess two. He passed gas on the way and his horse died of the smell."

He roared even harder. Every second gave Wayland more time to get the *Sea Cutter* ready to sail. "Guess again."

"Guess three. He was seeing your sweetheart and was afraid to come back."

"He was not seeing my sweetheart! I mean, I don't have a…! Humph. I'm going to the *Sea Cutter*."

My throat tightened. "I was just on my way to see Wayland. I can bring it to him."

He puffed out his chest. "The letter is addressed to Wayland and that's whom I am going to give it to."

"No!"

He looked at me, puzzled.

"I mean—I mean, he's not down at the *Sea Cutter*. He went over to the—to the church to pay his respects to my father. That's where I'm supposed to meet him."

"I'm much obliged, lad," he said in a gentle tone. "I'll walk there with you. I'd like to pay my respects to your good father too."

"Only I just remembered, I have to deliver a sextant to Isaiah Thornton. I'll meet you there."

I dashed for the door, then remembered the new letter to Mother and darted back to the counter.

"Here's another letter to my mother."

I sprinted out, looking back over my shoulder at Mr. Barton, and crashed into an apple cart. I went somersaulting over the top as the cart tumbled on its side, dumping apples all over me.

"Terribly sorry," I panted, struggling out of the heap.

"Sorry!" the apple dealer cried, grabbing me by my collar. "You'll be sorry when you've paid for these apples."

"No time. No time now." I wrenched free and tore down the street.

"Stop that boy!" the apple man cried.

I ran like a wild man, my sea bag bouncing in every direction. Everyone scattered as I careened around the corners, barely keeping my balance. A woman squealed as she leaped out of my way, tripped backward, and squished her bottom into a mud puddle.

"Sorry, Ma'am!"

My cap blew off but I didn't stop. When Mr. Barton didn't find Wayland at the church, he'd head straight to the *Sea Cutter*.

I got there just as Wayland was unfurling the mainsail. I could only gasp for breath.

"Goodness, Nat. Did you run the whole way?"

I nodded, leaped onto the *Sea Cutter* and raced to unlash the dock mooring lines.

"We can't cast off until we unfurl the sails," Wayland said, amused. "We're not in that much of a hurry. Sit down and take a breather."

"Sorry. Sorry. Too excited. Don't need rest. Unfurl

the sails!"

He put his hands on his hips. "Now, who's the captain here?"

"Sorry, Sir. Sorry. You're the captain."

"Then unfurl the sails, me mate."

"Aye, aye, Sir!"

I kept glancing down the dock, expecting to see Mr. Barton at any moment.

"Cast off," Wayland commanded.

I whipped the dock lines off the posts. Wayland hauled in the mainsail to catch the wind, and we were underway at last. Fifty yards from the docks I finally let out a sigh of relief.

"Wayland!" a voice boomed across the water. "Wayland! Put back in! Wayland! Important letter!"

I looked back, aghast, and saw Mr. Barton. I glanced at Wayland, but he was batting out the rustling mainsail and hadn't heard him.

I launched into an old song to drown out his shouting.

> *I'm bound for the open sea!*
> *It's a sailor's life for me!*
> *I'll not grow old on the land but bold*
> *I am to go to sea!*

"Quiet a moment." Wayland raised his hand. "Isn't that Mr. Barton on the dock? He's shouting something to us. My hearing's not as good as it used to be. What's he shouting?"

"He's shouting, 'Godspeed! Good voyage! Safe sailing!'"

"That's awfully decent of him to come see us off." He cupped his hands. "Godspeed to you too!"

Mr. Barton dropped his hands and stared after us without even scratching his bald head. Wayland waved at him cheerfully and soon we were far away from the docks.

"Strike up the next verse, my mate." He hauled in the mainsail further to steer the *Sea Cutter* at a fast point out of the harbor, the boat leaning to the leeward in a deep list.

With glee I sang the next verse and he joined in.

> *The wind and the foamy brine*
> *Forever will be mine!*
> *For I'd rather rot in a sailor's cot*
> *Than sleep in a palace fine!*

The *Sea Cutter* sailed out of the harbor and leaped like a stag over the ocean waves.

We were underway to find Father.

* * *

Father must've had the salt sea in his blood and passed it on to me, for I could feel my own blood sing in our rhythmic rise and fall over the sparkling swells that stretched in unbroken splendor to all horizons. The tang of the salt wind that whisked over my face was more delicious than the aroma of any spice. The splash of our bow, the snap and rustle of our sails, the creak of our mast, all seemed the loveliest music.

I saw a faraway look in Wayland's eyes and knew I need say nothing to him about the majesty of the sea. Our silence said more than any words.

As evening grew near, Wayland clinched the *Sea Cutter* onto a smooth southerly tack and stretched. "I believe I've grown a bit hungry, Nat."

"Me too. I'm starving."

"Then you best go down and fix us some grub or you'll be famished by the time you hit your hammock."

"So I'm elected ship's cook, am I?"

"On the spot."

"What about parliament? Even the King has parliament. Let's have a vote."

"That's fair. How do you cast your vote?"

"For you to be ship's cook."

"I cast my two votes for you to be ship's cook."

"Two votes! Why?"

"Because I'm the captain. Now you get down there and whip us up some grub, and it better be good or I'll make you walk the plank."

"I'm going. I'm going," I laughed.

After supper, we went topside. I lay on the bow to watch the sunset.

Red overwhelmed the sky and glowed off the towering clouds. Each moment the color became deeper, richer, softer. The sun itself seemed a soft blushing ball settling into the sea. There it melted, suffusing its liquid embers across the rolling waves. Blues, reds, purples, and greens played with each other in shifting, sliding patterns.

The sky mellowed to a deep dark blue, glimmering with stars. The blue surrendered to the true black of night and the stars grew to a brilliant canopy of piercing points of light, each radiant enough to outshine the diamonds on a king's crown. Heaped and scattered across the sky, they glowed as if part of an endless treasure.

A gibbous moon rose and stretched a silver path across the waters, like a trail leading to a land of enchantment. Wayland went below and lit a lantern that shone softly through the porthole of his quarters.

I stayed on the bow, my chin resting on my folded hands, and gazed at the silver trail until the rhythm of the waves offered to drift my soul to some timeless place from where all beauty came. The wind and waves heightened with the night, the *Sea Cutter* slicing through, whipping a chilling spray across my face.

I didn't care. Who cared about anything now? We were on our way to rescue Father.

At last I bid a farewell to the sea and sky and descended the companionway into Wayland's cabin, where he sat reading his Bible. He greeted me with a smile and a knowing nod, as if he too understood what I'd felt on my first night upon the sea. Then he returned to his reading.

I looked over his shoulder, and my eyes lit on a verse:

> There is a way that seemeth right
> unto a man, but the end thereof are the
> ways of death.

I jumped backward with a chill.

Wayland looked up. "Is something wrong?"

"No. Nothing." I wondered at my own reaction. "I'm going to hit my hammock."

"You've earned it. I'll sail through the night. You sail through the day tomorrow. Goodnight, my mate.

You're a true sailor now."

I tried to return the smile as I closed the door between Wayland's cabin and the galley. I groped my way through the galley and, closing the door to my cabin, climbed into my hammock by the moonlight shining through my porthole.

The rhythmic splash of the *Sea Cutter* slicing through the waves, and the creaking of the boat as she rocked, lulled me into sleep.

I woke with a start. A hand slapped over my mouth and I felt the cold steel of a blade pressed against my throat.

Above my head hung the oily face of Snake.

CHAPTER SEVEN
The Thing Below

A trickle of blood oozed down my neck.

"Don't call out," Snake hissed.

I nodded, terrified for my life.

He lifted my dagger from my throat and I clutched at the spot to staunch the blood.

"How did you get aboard?" I choked.

"My little lad, you might as well ask me how I do anything." He showed his crooked yellow teeth in a hollow laugh. I saw the opened hatch to the sail hold. "I can do whatever I want."

"You sure didn't find that map!"

He hit me across the face with the flat side of the

dagger.

"I don't need the map now, do I?" Drops of brown spittle came flying out in his rage. "You're going exactly where I want to go, so you can take me there."

I wiped the corner of my mouth where blood welled out.

"You already have a pearl worth a fortune."

"Nat, Nat, Nat, you jump to conclusions. You'll never be a good thinker like me. Who said I was going after pearls?"

"What do you want?"

His face contorted. "The Boar."

"The Boar?"

"A pirate captain. A mammoth, and his eyeteeth didn't stop growing 'til he had big tusks. He'll rip your throat out faster than a sword."

"He's at Perlas Grandes?"

"That's where he was heading when he went after me with those tusks. I dived overboard. I want revenge, and you're going to help me."

"Why me?"

"I need a child, and that's you, unless you want me to slice your heart out." He whipped the dagger to my chest, blood oozing under the point.

"You'll help me kill the Boar?"

I nodded, clenching my teeth.

"Good lad." He tousled my hair. I recoiled from his greasy touch. "We'll make our happy journey together. I'll stay quiet in the hold and you'll bring me food every night."

"We've only enough rations for two people."

"I don't mind eating yours. Are we agreed?"

A thought struck me. Once he was down in his hold, I could lock the hatch.

"Are we agreed?" He spit on his slimy hand.

"We're agreed." I spit on my own hand and held it out.

"I don't want to touch your spit!" he chortled, taking my chin in his hand. The putrid wetness of his spit smeared across my face.

"Just get down in the hold," I gagged.

"Gladly. It's nice and dark down there. Just my style." He wiped the rest of his stinking spit into my hair and started to climb down the hold.

I held my breath. Just a few more feet and I could slam the hatch shut and lock it.

He stopped, smirking. "You know, if I were you, I'd be thinking about locking me down here."

A jolt of despair shot through me.

"You won't do that, because I'd just pound on the hold until Wayland heard me, and then I'd show him this." He pulled out an envelope. "You tricked

Wayland into missing the letter your mother sent to him. Here's the letter your mother sent to *you*."

"How'd you get that?"

"As far as you're concerned, it might as well be magic. You know what your mother says in this letter, don't you? She forbids you to go to sea. Didn't I overhear Wayland say if he got such a message, that he'd turn around—even if you were halfway across the sea? Goodbye Father."

"How do I know that's the real letter?"

"Look."

Mother's handwriting covered the envelope, and I could catch the lovely faint scent of lavender that followed her around. He raised the letter out of the envelope an inch.

"Dear Nat," the first line read. "On no account do you have my approval to sail to Perlas Grandes...."

"Since I'll be with you for a while, we might as well learn how to get along," Snake said, pocketing the letter. "I don't think we'll have too much trouble considering how much we're alike."

"We're not at all alike!"

"Why not?"

"You're a thief and a liar."

"Hmm. Let's see. Was the pearl sent to you or to your mother?"

I remembered how I'd cracked open the pearl box. My cheeks burned.

"That makes you a thief, then, doesn't it? Wasn't there something else? A forged letter you gave to Wayland?"

I turned my head away.

"No answer? Too bad. I guess that makes you a liar."

I bit my lip.

"Nat. Nat," he said in mock kindness. "We've many leagues to sail together. We might as well be friends."

I turned my face back toward him with a look of scathing hatred.

"Why, good!" That terrible smile returned. "I do believe, my son, you're even starting to look like me. This will all go very well. Ta-ta, my little laddy."

With that he slid the rest of the way down into the hold. In a rage I leaped from my bunk and slammed the hatch shut, locking it with the steel bolt.

But what bolt could keep him from pounding on the floor and showing the letter to Wayland? In awful surrender, I slowly withdrew the bolt. It rasped as it slid, and I could hear Snake laughing.

* * *

The next morning I wore a kerchief around my neck to hide the dagger cut, and I picked at my food, pretending I wasn't hungry.

"Are you ill, Nat?" Wayland asked. "You haven't eaten a thing."

"Just a bit tired. I didn't sleep well."

"I hope you can stay awake sailing today." He stood and patted me on the back. "If you need me to sail a bit longer, I can."

"I'll be fine."

"Well, maybe I'll go topside with you for a while."

I sailed while he sat for an hour merely staring out across the ocean, his smiling eyes shining like the sun.

He didn't wake for lunch, which suited me fine, since he couldn't see I skipped mine. He did see me picking at my dinner, even though I was starving by this time. He knit his brow, but said nothing.

In the dead of night Snake came out to eat and then kept me awake ranting about the Boar.

The next morning dark rings hung under my eyes, and my stomach had tied itself into a painful knot, but I still hardly ate any breakfast.

Wayland frowned. "All right, Nat, tell me what's going on."

"Nothing!" I looked up, wide-eyed.

"Don't say that. You haven't been eating."

"I guess—I guess I'm seasick."

"Seasick! 'Tis odd. I never would've thought it of you, with all the salt sea in your blood. You look tired

too. Maybe 'tis not seasickness. Maybe we should sail home and find you a doctor."

"No! I'll get over it."

"All right, but I best keep an eye on you."

As we sailed from the North Atlantic into the South Atlantic, I comforted myself by studying the map of Perlas Grandes, daydreaming about Father. I studied it so often, I memorized the route, then burned the map to keep it from Snake. He came out to eat my food each night while raging against the Boar. I got thinner, the rings under my eyes grew darker, and Wayland looked more worried.

*   *   *

On the tenth morning after we'd sailed into the South Atlantic, clouds gathered on the horizon. If only it would rain! I could drink my fill without worrying about saving most of my water ration for Snake.

"I don't like the look of those clouds," Wayland said.

"Why?"

"They look dangerous."

"How can you tell—" Streaks of silver flashed past me.

"Flying fish! Knock them down, Nat. Knock them down. They're good eating." He swatted one into the cockpit, where it flopped around madly.

Extra food! I slapped one. "Got him!"

"You're way behind. I just got two at once."

We danced around like whirling dervishes, our cockpit filling with slippery fish.

"Sorry!" I panted, after I slapped a fish that hit him on the nose.

"Think nothing of it," he said, rubbing his nose.

As soon as I turned away, something struck the back of my head.

"Oh, sorry." Wayland feigned innocence. "I was knocking a fish out of your hair."

I became more careful where I flung my hands.

Soon flopping fish covered our cockpit and we were laughing like a couple of maniacs, each trying to outdo the other.

The *Sea Cutter* gave a mighty quiver, as if something massive had rubbed against our hull. I froze. Wayland froze too, staring wide-eyed down at the deck as if he wanted to see through the boat into the sea.

"There's something big down there. I should've known these fish were flying to get away from danger."

The *Sea Cutter* shuddered again, a long, deep tremor. We stumbled, clutching at the rigging.

"What is it?"

"I have an idea, but I hope I'm wrong. I hope it's just a big shark."

"Just a big—"

Something gave a forceful bump to our hull, knocking us off our feet. Then all was still. Terrifying images filled my head and, like Wayland, I hoped it was just a big shark.

"Look!" He pointed past our stern. "It's as I feared."

A massive black mountain rose out of the water, twice as big as the *Sea Cutter*, sheets of green water cascading down its monstrous sides. With a dull roar, an enormous spume of water erupted from his head.

"A whale," I breathed.

"Not just a whale. A sperm whale, and a male at that."

"A male?"

"Look at the size of his head. They use them to fight each other, and to crush ships. They can take down a ship three times their own size with that battering ram."

"Is that what he was doing down there?"

"Not a bit," Wayland laughed dryly. "Testing our size, no doubt. If he'd rammed us, the *Sea Cutter* would be nothing but splinters."

The whale sounded with majestic slowness, the slap of the huge fluke spraying us with freezing salt water as he dived.

"Hold on tight."

"What good will that do? If he hits the *Sea Cutter*,

I'll just be holding onto a scrap of wood."

"And that scrap of wood might save your life."

"I doubt it."

Wayland grabbed my shoulders and shook me, with fire in his eyes. "Never, never, never surrender the chance to live. To live only a few more minutes. As long as you live, there's hope."

I gulped and clutched onto a spar. "If I don't make it, promise you'll take care of Mother."

Wayland grit his teeth. "If I make it, I'm going to make darned sure you make it."

I could see the whale in my mind's eye, rushing up faster and faster.

"The Lord is my shepherd; I shall not want," Wayland recited. "He maketh me to lie down in green pastures: he leadeth me beside the still waters."

I pictured the whale turning slightly to aim his battering ram at our hull.

"He restoreth my soul. He leads me in the paths of righteousness for his name's sake."

I squeezed my eyes shut.

"Yea, though I walk through the shadow of the valley of death—"

An explosion shattered the prayer.

CHAPTER EIGHT
A Fight for Life

The colossal black column erupted toward the sky. Sheets of green seawater cascaded from its sides, drenching us. Still the whale rose, towering toward the top of our mast. It hung regally in the air in proud display.

"Hold on! It's coming down."

With a deafening boom, the whale crashed back into the sea. The splash knocked my breath out, sweeping my feet from the deck while I clung to the spar. The *Sea Cutter* reeled sideways, her cockpit filling halfway with water.

Then all was still. Wayland and I were exchanging glances of bemusement when the whale rose and swam beside us, watching us with a small black eye.

It was as if he was waiting for us to do something that

equaled his leap. At last, with what I thought was a look of disappointment, maybe even disgust in his eyes, he turned and swam away.

"Why, God be praised." Wayland laughed in relief. "He only wanted someone to play with."

"Some game. I'm glad he didn't want to play tag."

A flying fish leaped from our half-flooded cockpit back into the sea.

"There's enough water for the fish to fly out!" Three more escaped as Wayland spoke. "Catch them. Knock them on the head."

We floundered and slid around the cockpit, trying to grab the fish in the water, but they were quick and slippery.

"Got one." He slammed its head against the bench.

"Me too. Whoa!"

Splash. I fell right on my butt. I didn't think that was funny, but Wayland did.

By the time the last fish had streaked out to the gray choppy waves, we'd managed to catch a good bucketful. My stomach growled.

"Watch out!"

The wind, shifting from starboard to port, swept the *Sea Cutter*'s boom across the cockpit. I ducked just in time. The sail whipped back to starboard, and I ducked again. Wayland unleashed the tiller so he could

navigate the changing gusts.

"Go cook us those fish." He studied the black clouds. "We need to eat them before the storm hits."

Lightning flashed in the clouds, but nothing was going to get in the way of my eating. I fried those fish quickly, drank a pitcher of water, and ran topside. I gulped down my food twice as fast as Wayland, then stared at his plate.

"I'm full," he said, handing it to me. "Could you finish these?"

I gobbled them down in a flash.

"'Tis great getting over your seasickness even in this rough ocean. I always knew you had the salt sea in your blood. Are you ready to fit the *Sea Cutter* for the storm? I can't take my hand off the tiller with these winds."

"What's first?" I sprang to my feet, feeling like a new boy.

"We need to reef the mainsail. The less canvas we show to the wind, the less it can push us around. Leave the jib. That'll give me the little bit of wind I need to steer the *Sea Cutter* straight into the waves."

I unlashed the mainsail line from its cleat and began reefing the sail, folding the canvas onto the boom as it came down, but I hadn't gone far before the line hit a snag and refused to move.

"You'll have to climb the mast and see what's happened," Wayland said.

I leaped upon the rigging and scrambled up the pitching mast like a monkey, the rocking boat tilting me over the black water.

"The whale's splash jammed a piece of flotsam in the block!" I hollered down over the winds. I yanked it free, then saw something that raised the hair on my neck. I raced down the mast.

"The starboard shroud is fraying."

The shrouds kept the mast from tumbling down like a tent pole that's pulled loose.

"We'll have to replace it."

I scampered back up with a coil of line over my shoulder, which I lashed to the top of the mast. I leapt from rigging to rigging, coming down to lash the shroud at the bottom, winching it tight before I threw the knot.

"Go up and cut the old one free."

I scuttled up again and cut the old shroud. It snapped with a crack like a pistol.

When I reached the deck, Wayland took the back of my neck in one hand and pressed his forehead against mine.

"You've shown me you're a real sailor, Nat. But even if you weren't, you'd still be my favorite boy."

I blushed, half in embarrassment, half in pleasure, while he squeezed the back of my neck.

"I want you to go down and get some sleep until the storm hits. You see this line? Tie it next to the

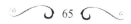

companionway. When you're ready to come topside, reach out to that line and tie it around your waist before you come out. The waves are going to be big, and 'tis for your own safety in case you get washed overboard."

"What about your own line?" I tied mine at the companionway.

"I have the tiller to hang onto. Go get some sleep. You'll find a bell in my third drawer. 'Tis a little trick for new sailors. Hang it above your hammock. When the sea gets really rough, it'll ring and wake you. That's when I'll need your help."

I went below and hung the bell, then collapsed across my hammock and fell asleep within moments.

I dreamed I was five years old, sitting on my child's rocking chair, swaying back and forth. The evening bell rang rhythmically—time for Wayland to share dinner with us. He came and held out his calloused hand to help me from the rocking chair, but I couldn't reach out to take it. An invisible wall separated us, and my happiness disappeared.

The dream turned into a nightmare. I clung onto a bucking horse while the town crier rang his bell loud and fast, crying, "Hear ye. Hear ye. Nat fails to tell Wayland about Snake. Wayland is dead." *Ring! Ring! Ring!*

I woke in blackness, the *Sea Cutter* tossing every which way, while the bell rang with a mad clatter.

Lightening flashed and thunder roared. I'd left Wayland alone to sail the storm!

I dashed up the companionway, forgetting to tie the line about me, just as a vicious wave broke over the *Sea Cutter.*

"Nat!" Wayland let go of the tiller and leaped toward me.

A freezing giant hand slapped my body off the boat, knocking my air out. It crashed me down into the roiling water, twisting and turning me as if it were a cat playing with a mouse. Fireworks exploded in my lungs.

I kicked and clawed at the wave, but it sank me head over heels. The fireworks turned to cannon shot. In another moment I'd breathe water.

A line rasped across my side and I grabbed it.

I flew yards in the air, the *Sea Cutter* yanking me out of the wave. I drew in a breath like a bellows. The line thrashed down into the trough of a wave, then flung me in the air again, the furious giant snapping his whip to flick me off.

I held on, my hands burning, my shoulders aching, the ocean plowing into my face, the rain pouring over me. Lightning flashed, and I caught a glimpse of the *Sea Cutter.*

"Wayland! Wayland!" I screamed.

He couldn't hear me above the roaring waves and wind.

I pulled myself forward on the whipping line inch by inch, until one wave finally bruised me into the *Sea Cutter*'s side.

"Wayland!" No answer. He wasn't pointing the *Sea Cutter's* bow into the waves. She broached aimlessly, the waves hitting her at dangerous angles.

One banged me against the side of the boat so hard that for a moment all was a spinning darkness. Another smack like that would knock the line from my grasp.

I pulled myself upward, crying "Ah!" at the top of my lungs, and with a last effort tumbled over the gunwale just as a bolt of lightning made everything brighter than day.

The tiller thrashed from side to side.

Wayland was gone.

CHAPTER NINE
Snake's Idea

A wave crashed over the side of the *Sea Cutter*, tipping her far sideways, almost sinking her. I hung onto a cleat while the seawater frothed knee-deep over the deck.

Barrelfuls of seething black water sloshed through the hatchway where I'd foolishly dashed out. I slogged through the roiling water and forced the hatch closed, then floundered to the tiller, grabbing it to struggle the bow of the *Sea Cutter* straight into the waves.

"Wayland!" Another flash of lightning showed no hands clinging to the boat, no line trailing over the gunwale.

Maybe he's swimming nearby! I tried to wipe the stinging, lashing rain out of my eyes as I searched the

empty sinister waters. The lump of ice in my chest had nothing to do with the freezing seawater spraying over me. If he'd gone overboard, the sea had swept him far away.

"Wayland!" I choked.

A sheer cliff of water raced toward me. I forced the bow to point into it. The *Sea Cutter* plowed into the wave as if she meant to go right under it, but the bow struggled up, shuddering, creaking, groaning, lifting a massive cascade of water and throwing it backward like a fine horse leaping out of a river and shaking the water from its mane. With her nose up, she fought her way like a thoroughbred to the crest.

"Wayland," I sobbed as I battled the waves.

A hundred images flashed before me. Wayland giving me an elaborate wooden model of a schooner and helping me assemble it. Wayland stretching his long legs across the floor in a V as I tried running back and forth without getting caught in them, and screaming with laughter when he did catch and tickle me.

A bolt of lightning and the realization hit at the same moment: He'd died with a lie between us. The lightning seemed to sear my heart.

"I wish I'd told you. I wish I'd told you," I moaned.

All night I grappled with the tempest—wave after

wave after wave, until it seemed I'd sailed the storm all my life.

I thought of myself as a small boat on a tossing ocean. *You stay afloat by facing right into the waves*, I thought, *like telling the truth straight on.*

I hadn't done so with Wayland, and now I'd never be able to mend that breach.

At dawn, light began to filter through the clouds. The storm broke up faster than it had gathered. Within an hour, the waves lessened and the sky cleared.

Numb with fatigue and grief, I lashed the tiller to an even course and opened the main hatch.

Wayland lay wedged at an odd angle on his desk.

"Wayland!" I leaped all the way down the companionway.

He made no reply.

I grabbed his arm, shaking him. "Wayland! Wayland!"

His eyes opened, unfocused at first. "Nat, you're alive. I thought you got washed overboard."

"I hung on to that line!"

"Ow, my head!" He winced, putting his hand to a purple bruise. "I fell down the companionway when I lunged for you. I must've landed right on my head, and the tossing must've thrown me up here."

I helped him from his desk to his hammock, where

he looked out the porthole.

"Now it's morning and the storm's over. You sailed through the storm yourself?"

I blushed with embarrassed pleasure.

"Well done!" He shook my hand, then he chucked me under the chin. "Now if we can just keep you from going topside without going swimming, we might make a sailor of you."

"Perhaps I should teach you how to go down into your cabin. Going feet first is the usual method."

"Well, I wouldn't have fallen if I'd had something to hang onto. Like your hair!" He grabbed at my hair, but I ducked back laughing.

"You'll have to be faster than that, old salt."

He groaned and lay back.

I bent over him. "What is it?"

Before I knew it, he caught me by the hair. "I may not be as quick as you, but I'm smarter." He tickled me. "Say 'uncle.'"

"Uncle! Uncle!" I squealed, until he let go. "I'll fix some food and coffee. I'm famished."

"Me too."

I lit the stove, ground some coffee, and cooked a rasher of salt pork for each of us, which I served with hardtack. We wolfed it down, then enjoyed our full bellies while we talked about my adventures with the storm.

"You need rest," I said. "I'll go topside and sail. You lie back here. Try to sleep."

"Nay. I need to check over the *Sea Cutter*. See what damage she sustained."

"You just hit your head!"

"Nat, this isn't the first time I've been knocked on the head and gotten back to work as soon as I woke. Sailing has made me a tough nut. You've been up all night. Go get some sleep."

I could've said, *Wait a minute*, and told him about Snake, but was now the right time? No. I'd lock the hatch, get some sleep, and let him recover from his fall first.

But when I opened the door to my cabin, Snake was crawling out. He held no dagger and, glancing round at me, his hand flew to the sheath. I launched through the air to collide with his chest, wrapping my arms around his like a vise.

He cursed, squirming to free his arm. Sweat streamed into my eyes while I struggled to hold him, but I couldn't. His tattooed arm yanked free and in a flash he pulled the dagger. I grabbed his wrist.

He bit my hands, pummeling me with his free fist. I ignored the pain, but he was stronger than I, and I could feel his greasy wrist slipping out of my grip.

The dagger hand broke free and I ducked as he whipped it through the air to slice my throat.

I came back up with a punch to his chin that had all the strength of my legs in it. His head snapped back, the dagger flying out of his hands.

I dove for the dagger, but he kicked me in the stomach, doubling me over. The *Sea Cutter* rocked as he grabbed for it, and the dagger slid away from his grip.

I sprang on his back. He shook me off and punched my head twice. Everything swirled. I swung back, but he was a fighter, and I wasn't. He easily avoided my swing and punched me in the stomach. When I doubled over again, he hit my chin with his knee and spat in my face.

I needed to get in closer where the fight wasn't about punches. I threw myself onto Snake, using my last strength to try to wrestle him down. We staggered back and forth with the rocking of the boat until she rolled deeply, with the tilt to my back.

I twisted, putting the tilt to his back, and did the only fighting move that I knew. A child's trick, really. I put my leg behind Snake's ankles, pushing him backward. He tripped, cracked his head against the cabin wall, and went limp.

Before he could recover, I tied him from head to toe.

I stood over his unconscious body catching my breath, feeling grim triumph. Now when I told Wayland about him, he'd already be captive.

He slobbered curses as he woke, uselessly struggling against the line pinning his arms and legs.

"I suppose you're going to throw me overboard."

"I'm no murderer. I'm going to show you to Wayland and we'll turn you over to the authorities for hanging."

"You can't do that! I'll tell him about the letter."

"I'm going to tell him anyway."

His tone changed to a whine. "It's too bad things ended up this way. You want to go to Perlas Grandes to find your father, which you can't do if you tell Wayland about me. Maybe we could work out a way where you wouldn't have to tell."

"I'm going to tell."

"We've just been through a storm. He might want to put into a port to make repairs. You could sneak me off the *Sea Cutter* and still find your father."

I didn't speak, thinking, and then shook my head. "I'm going topside to tell Wayland about you now."

I slid my dagger under my mattress and tipped Snake headfirst into the hold. He fell with a satisfying *thunk* and another curse. I slammed the hatch and locked it.

I went topside and found Wayland inspecting the *Sea*

Cutter.

"Not sleeping?"

"I couldn't." *Wayland, I have something to tell you* was on the tip of my tongue, but instead I asked, "How's she doing? Serious damage?"

"The tiller's pretty loose. We'll need to make repairs."

An unpleasant but driving spark ignited in my stomach.

"You think we might have to put into a port?"

"'Tis always a good idea after a storm, but I think we can make these repairs at sea."

"If it's better to put into port, why don't we do that?" My breath felt hot with the blaze that spread through me.

"It'd take us a week or so out of schedule. I thought you wanted to try to find Perlas Grandes as soon as you could."

"We had talked about me seeing a doctor." The words burned. "I still don't feel well. I could see a doctor if we went into port."

"My goodness, Nat." He slapped his forehead. "You sailed so well I thought you must've recovered. Of course we'll put into port. I reckon we're east of Brazil, closest to the port of Recife. I'll take a bearing tonight."

Snake's idea will work, I told myself, my face blazing.

I should've known he had a different plan.

CHAPTER TEN
The Grip of Death

After dinner, I snuck into the hold.

"We're sailing to Recife. I'll leave you there. Where's the letter?"

"It's hidden—my insurance you won't tell Wayland about me. I'll tell you where it is when you let me go."

I fetched a lantern to search Snake and the hold, but I found no letter. I felt so exhausted I could hardly keep my eyes open. I locked the hatch and fell into my hammock.

The next day, Wayland whistled as he worked, but I couldn't meet his eye.

In the night I had to go into the hold and feed the greasy, drooling worm with a spoon since he was bound with line. I couldn't wait to get rid of the loathsome monster.

On the eighth day of sailing westward, a screech of gulls flew by.

"Land ho!" Wayland called.

A strip of darkness lay along the horizon—the coast of South America. The waters turned from gray to lovely blues and greens.

Soon we encountered fishing vessels painted red and yellow and violet, full of men with skin every shade of brown. Some boats passed near enough to shout greetings in Portuguese. Our small craft with two white men aroused their curiosity.

"De onde vocês viajar de navio?" they shouted.

Wayland said they wanted to know from where we'd sailed.

"Nós viemos de navio de New Bedford," he shouted back.

They whistled and clapped. *"Muito bem. Muito bem. Você é um homem corajoso!"*

"They say we're brave."

They sailed alongside us, wanting to know how we'd survived the storm. Wayland pointed to me, telling them I had sailed us through it. They cheered and applauded. My ears burned.

"Tell them about the whale."

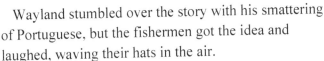

Wayland stumbled over the story with his smattering of Portuguese, but the fishermen got the idea and laughed, waving their hats in the air.

As we sailed into the harbor, we saw boats carrying mounds of green bananas, piles of oranges, and burlap sacks of beans. We passed skiffs full of violet, pink, orange, and deep yellow flowers. The sun shone with warm friendliness on everyone, sparkling on water that was a hundred shades of green.

Rounding a point, we saw Recife, its white houses shining against the tropical green hills.

We dropped anchor, and an ancient man in a blue-checkered shirt and a yellow kerchief rowed his purple and red dinghy out to meet us, offering to rent it to us. We agreed.

"The first thing is to find someone who speaks English to act as our translator," Wayland said. "Go ashore and see who you can find."

I rowed the ancient man to the docks, but when we reached the pier dozens of clamoring, curious children greeted me. They pushed each other aside for a chance to pinch my white skin, squealing with delight when they found it felt just like their own.

They shouted questions to me in Portuguese. When they realized that I didn't understand they shouted louder, as if this would force the meaning upon me.

A handsome, chocolate-brown boy about my age stepped forward. He wore a frayed white cotton shirt and patched white pants over bare feet. He quieted the children with a wave of his hand, looking me up and down with dark, intelligent eyes.

"Where do you come from?" he asked me in perfect English.

"We came from New Bedford," I answered, overcoming my surprise.

"In that boat? All the way?"

"Yes. And we were in the storm too."

The boy told the children, and they began again to clamor.

"They say you are brave." Dozens of shining eyes gave me friendly compliments.

"How do you say 'thank you?'"

"*Obrigado*."

"*Obrigado*," I told the grinning faces.

"What is your name?"

"Nat. What's yours?"

"My name is Paulo."

I shook his hand. "Pleased to meet you, Paulo."

"I am also pleased."

Cheers and whistles broke out, one boy even standing on his head. Then there was nothing for it. I had to shake hands with each of them while saying,

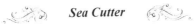

"Pleased to meet you." They imitated Paulo, saying, "I am also pleased." More often than not it came out like "I emey aldwa pezo," or something equally meaningless.

"Why are you here?" Paulo asked.

"To make repairs. The rudder worked loose in the storm."

"I help repair boats. Take me to your captain."

"All right. He'll be glad to meet you."

I rowed Paulo toward the *Sea Cutter*. Along the way we saw a man rowing a donkey, and we both laughed so hard we almost rolled the dinghy over.

When we reached the *Sea Cutter*, I introduced Paulo to Wayland.

"Why, he's a good find, Nat." He shook Paulo's hand. "What do you get for wages?"

"There is no need to pay me. Nat is my friend." He then surprised both of us by diving off the stern.

"What's he doing?" Wayland asked.

"I told him we had a problem with the rudder."

We waited for him to surface. "I'm going in after him!" Wayland ripped off his boots.

Paulo's grinning face broke the water. "It is going to be easy. No wood is broken, but both bolts are loose. Give me a wrench."

"How do you stay underwater so long?"

"Many of us grew up diving for a living." He dove underwater with the wrench.

After two minutes he came back up, his white teeth gleaming. "All done."

Wayland felt the tiller. "Solid as a rock. I don't know how to thank you, Paulo. Do you think your parents would mind if you stayed for dinner?"

"I have no parents. I would like to stay for dinner."

After dinner Paulo took me back to Recife. Crowds milled around with people selling their wares on the sidewalks.

One man carried a big parrot with yellow, orange, scarlet, and green feathers. It talked to everyone. Another had a monkey that clambered all over him, then peeked out from behind the man's back when people came over.

Sacks of spices filled the air with heady fragrances. Musicians played strange rhythms while women in billowing, brightly colored skirts whirled in dances among spinning fireworks. Recife was like a land of magic that made New Bedford seem stark and gray.

Paulo and I liked to look at the same curiosities in sidewalk shops, and we both laughed at the same things. The longer we talked, the more we laughed.

The gentle blue of evening fell. "I have an idea. Why don't you sleep on the boat tonight?"

"That would be fun."

When Paulo assured Wayland there was nobody expecting him, he was happy to welcome my new friend aboard for the night. He gave Paulo a long, thoughtful look as we went down the companionway.

"Do you want to know a secret?" I asked in our cabin. "We're sailing to Perlas Grandes!"

"What an adventure. Then you think it's real?"

"Do you?"

"I don't see why not. Some people say we know every foot of the ocean, so there can't be any Perlas Grandes. But it seems to me the ocean is much too big for us to ever know every part."

I told him about Father.

"I hope you find your father. I do not remember my parents. English missionaries raised me."

"I'm sorry."

Our talk paused, until I said, "A donkey in a boat!" and we both burst out laughing.

There comes a certain time of night when everything seems funny. At one point, Paulo was imitating how I looked sailing in the storm, while I rolled in my hammock in tears.

Yet even as I rolled in laughter, a part of me could not forget my deadly secret. Paulo didn't know that below his feet lay a killer.

*   *   *

In the morning, Wayland shook us awake for steak and eggs.

"Whom do you live with?" he asked Paulo over coffee afterwards.

"I don't live with anyone."

"Have you ever thought of going to sea?"

I held my breath.

"I often think of it."

"If I know Nat, then you already know where we're going. It's dangerous, but I'm going to make it as safe as possible. If you wish, it would be an honor if you would join us." He held out his hand.

Paulo took it, smiling. "I would like that."

"Hooray!"

"Good. Good. I'm hiring you as crew, so if you don't accept payment, I can't take you."

Paulo nodded shyly.

"Excellent. So we need to get you sailing clothes, and this morning it's off to find a doctor."

"Are you sick?" I asked him.

"No. I thought you were." He looked puzzled.

"Oh yes. A doctor."

"Do you know of a good doctor?" Wayland asked Paulo.

Paulo nodded. Wayland gave us money for the

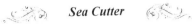
doctor and for Paulo's clothes, and sent us on our way.

"You don't look sick to me." Paulo gave me a keen look as we rowed to the dock.

"No."

"You lied to Wayland?"

I nodded.

"That's not good."

"It's too hard to explain, but I don't need a doctor."

I purchased a cheap bottle of murky green liquid from a potions man, which I planned to dump overboard little by little, and we bought sailing gear for Paulo.

We spent the rest of the money on candied fruits and cakes. We finished with flaky buns dipped in honey so sweet it made my teeth hurt.

"It looks as if we can sail with the morning tide," Wayland said when we returned. "If the doctor thinks you're well enough."

"Oh, yes. He said I just have an upset stomach."

"We know that! We want to know why."

"He said it was upset because I wasn't feeling well."

Wayland opened his mouth to speak, but I rushed on. "He said this medicine would make it all better."

"It looks full. You haven't taken any yet."

"Uh, I—"

"Take some right now."

"But—"

"Right now!"

I opened the bottle and a sickly sour smell hit my nose. I brought the bottle to my lips and swallowed the tiniest bit.

My stomach turned into a throbbing knot and I wanted to vomit.

"That was just a sip! Take your medicine, Nat."

I closed my eyes and took a gulp. The throbbing in my stomach tripled and pulsated all the way up my throat. I ran to the side of the *Sea Cutter* and threw up all my sweets.

Wayland scratched his head. "'Tis a strange cure."

"It's supposed…supposed to clean me out."

"It does that all right. Are you both ready to prepare for the morning tide?"

"Yes!" We slapped each other's backs.

I'd get rid of Snake, and have a friend aboard.

In the morning, I snuck into the galley and rubbed a bit of soot into our kerosene valve. The burner no longer lit, but it'd be easy for me to fix.

"Wayland." I stuck my head above board. "The stove isn't working."

"Well, by the sea serpent. We can't sail like that."

Both he and Paulo came down to the galley to examine the stove.

"No room for three," I said. "I'll inspect the boat again."

I disappeared into my cabin, opened the hatch, and crawled down to Snake.

"Now's the time," I whispered, slitting his bonds.

With my dagger at his back, I made him climb topside and drove him to the side of the *Sea Cutter*.

"Tell me where you hid the letter, then jump off."

He turned around and folded his arms with a cocky expression. "I've changed my mind."

"You can't change your mind!"

"I can't swim. I'd rather face Wayland."

"You're not going to see Wayland."

"I could shout for him."

"Go over." I held the dagger to his chest.

"You see, Nat," he grinned, "we are alike. You're ready to drown a man. You're a murderer like me."

"I'm not at all like you!" I hit him across the jaw with the flat of the dagger.

His head snapped back, his eyes rolled up, and he fell backward into the water. A minute passed.
Three. Five. He didn't rise.

My fury vanished. What had I done? I'd knocked a man out, sending him to die.

A pistol shot rang, an impact hitting my back. Time slowed. My dagger fell, flipping leisurely. Then the green water slowly came to meet me as I tumbled over. The sunlit roof of water closed above me like slow curtains. The bullet in my back throbbed as I sank deeper into the darkness.

Then I remembered what lay at the bottom of that darkness—Snake's corpse. My foot hit sand and, terrified, I shoved myself upward.

A cold dead hand gripped my ankle.

The last of my air went out in a silent scream.

CHAPTER ELEVEN
Perlas Grandes

"Let the water out!" Paulo commanded me. Someone pushed hard on my chest.

I choked out water, spluttering but breathing.

"Good work!" Paulo shouted.

"You're going to be all right, lad." Wayland wiped his forehead.

"It's no good," I wheezed, with what I imagined were my dying breaths. "I've been shot in the back."

"What? Roll him over. Yes, there's a bloody rip in your shirt." Wayland tore the shirt open. "That's strange. The wound looks as if the bullet bounced right off your back." He laughed. "That was no pistol, Nat. The shroud you rigged on the mast snapped. The end of the line must've whipped over and hit you."

I felt stronger and sat up, glancing at Paulo. He was trying not to laugh.

"We rushed topside when the shroud broke and didn't see you. Paulo dove in and found you."

I looked down at my ankle, wrapped in a tentacle of seaweed. The hand that had gripped me. The snapped shroud lay on the deck, and my stomach turned.

"The shroud didn't snap. Someone cut it."

Wayland frowned. "Who'd do that?"

Snake. I jumped to my feet.

"We can rig that shroud fast, can't we, Paulo?"

"There's no rush, my lad," Wayland said.

"Yes there is." I stared over the harbor. It no longer seemed a bright, lovely place to me, but a place of ominous threats.

"Come on, Paulo."

I worked the top while Paulo worked the bottom to rig the new shroud. As we finished, I saw a small racing boat speeding toward us.

"Hoist the sails!" I yelled.

"Now who's captain around here?"

"I'm sorry, Wayland. Please believe me, we have to get out of here."

"Why?"

"No time now! Please!"

"All right. Hoist the sails. Raise the anchor."

We were underway, but the *Sea Cutter* felt awkward, as if dragging something, while the small boat gained on us.

"What's that drag?" asked Wayland.

A shot. A giant black-haired man in the fast boat brandished a pistol, commanding us to stop.

Wayland grabbed the tiller from Paulo. He pointed the *Sea Cutter* into the wind and away from the racing boat, close-hauling the sails until the boat was heeling sideways and bubbling the water as she gathered speed.

"They're trying to head us off at the mouth of the harbor. Their boat is too small to chase us on the open sea. Prepare to jibe."

Wayland shoved the tiller and the mainsail swung across the boat with a lightning-fast lurch. Paulo and I threw ourselves to the deck to keep from being killed by the sudden sweep of the boom.

The racing boat changed tack by coming about, a slower but safer way to turn, so we pulled ahead.

Both boats struck out toward the harbor's mouth, but the *Sea Cutter* wouldn't fly, and the other boat gained on us again.

"Paulo, take the tiller. Nat, grab the mainsheet. I want to find what's causing our drag."

I seized the taut mainsheet and wound it around my

hand so I could pull on the mainsail better, but I fell over as the sheet went slack and the mainsail swung out wildly. Someone had cut the line.

The racing boat pulled alongside us and the black-haired man leaped in, grabbing me from behind while holding the pistol to my head.

"What do you want?" Wayland demanded. "If it's the boat or me, take it. Leave the boys alone."

"That up to new captain." He stared at the side of the boat.

A pale hand gripped the gunwale, then another, holding my dagger.

"Snake!" exclaimed Wayland, as the villain slithered over the edge. "Don't hurt the boys. Take whatever you want. Leave the boys alone."

"Cease the orders, former captain. I'll do as I want."

"What do you want?"

"To have you take me to Perlas Grandes."

"How did you find us?"

"I've been aboard all along, but I couldn't have done it without Nat. He hid me from you."

Wayland shot me a questioning look, but I lowered my eyes.

"Robo," Snake commanded the brutish man. "Please escort this gentleman down to the sail hold and lock him in."

When Robo dragged me backward, Wayland and
Paulo started toward me. Robo stopped, cocking the
pistol so that just a twitch of his finger would put a
bullet in my brain. They both froze.

"You and your Brazilian boy might not wish to
interfere," Snake said. "As long as we hold Nat, you'll
sail us to Perlas Grandes and do whatever other little
things we want."

With that Robo wrapped his arm around my neck,
pulled me up so my feet kicked at the ground, carried
me down to my cabin, and threw me into the foul sail
hold.

It turned pitch black as he slammed the hatch and
threw the lock with a loud *ker-chunk.*

* * *

Hours passed. My heart reeled with shame from the
danger in which I'd placed Wayland and Paulo. I beat
my fist against my forehead but could think of no plan.
Snake held all the cards.

No. Wait. I held an ace.

Someone threw the bolt, and Snake's leering face
glowed above a lantern.

"Tables have turned now." The stink grew worse
as he climbed down.

"What will you do with Wayland and Paulo?"

"Have them sail me to my revenge." He grinned with

all his crooked teeth.

"They can't."

His face fell. "What do you mean?"

"They'll never make it through the reefs."

"You have a map—"

"I burned it."

His hideous face turned purple. "Burned it?"

"I memorized it first. You'll never get on or off Perlas Grandes without my help."

He knocked me over, holding the dagger to my throat. "You'll help!"

"Kill me, and you'll never reach Perlas Grandes."

He paused.

"You're willing to get this close to your father and leave him behind?"

"I don't believe you ever planned to rescue him."

Snake scowled and let me rise.

"All right. We'll rescue him then, as soon as you help me kill the Boar."

I shook my head. "I'm not killing anyone."

Snake grabbed my shirtfront, sticking his repulsive face in mine. "You want to trade the life of the Boar for the lives of Wayland and Paulo?"

I gulped. He had me. "You'll help me rescue Father?"

"You'll help me kill the Boar?"

I nodded. "But if you don't save Father or you hurt my friends, I won't help you off the island."

"We'll rescue your father," he said in disgust, and released me.

I rubbed my chest. "What's your plan for the Boar?"

His face twisted in hate. "We'll ambush him. You jump in front of him to distract him, and I'll stab him from behind."

"You said you needed a child. Why?"

"Can you imagine his surprise when a child jumps in front of him? If I took Robo, the Boar wouldn't hesitate to charge. I need that moment of hesitation."

"If he doesn't hesitate, he'll kill me. You're putting me in the most dangerous—"

"Danger! What about the danger I'll face when I sneak on land looking for your father—if the Boar hasn't killed him yet."

I lurched and clutched Snake's sleeve. "Killed him?" Why hadn't I thought of that?

"Or captured him. The Boar's crew needs slaves."

"Not dead?"

"I can't answer until I've scouted." He frowned, rising and pulling himself from the hold. He turned back to me, his face enraged. "Of all the stubborn brats in the world, I had to get you." He slammed and locked the hatch.

In the darkness, I couldn't stop imagining scenes of the Boar's tusks ripping out Father's throat. Robo brought me hardtack and water each night, but I lost track of time. The Boar's tusks dripping with gore, Wayland and Paulo, my guilt, the Boar's dripping tusks —my mind whirled around until the maelstrom made me thrash my head against the hull.

*　*　*

The hatch opened, evening sunshine half blinding me. I shielded my eyes.

"Come topside," Snake ordered.

I stumbled after him. Robo held the tiller and mainsheet.

"Where are Wayland and Paulo?"

"Below."

"Wayland!" I called.

"He's gagged."

"Why?"

"So he can't call for help. Can you imagine what the Boar's crew would do if they found us?"

"We're that close?"

"We will be soon. Look." He pointed east to a strip of darkness on the horizon. "They said it didn't exist, but there it is. The coast of Perlas Grandes."

CHAPTER TWELVE
Snake's Revenge

My pulse pounded through every bit of my body.
Perlas Grandes!

"Father," I whispered.

"If he's still alive." Snake mocked me.

That snapped me back. I had to know.

"Let's go in," I said.

"We stand off until the full moon."

"Why not now?"

"Because of the Boar. Best we sneak in at night."

I had to grit my teeth through the long sunset and the
slow moonrise.

"Can we sail in now?" I pleaded.

"What's first?"

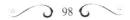

"To find the white marble cliffs."

I took the tiller and sailed along the string of reefs, looking at the distant island until I saw massive white cliffs shining in the moonlight.

"Now we sail until we come to the first shipwreck and pass it to starboard, for a hidden reef lies to port." The top of a mast jabbed out of the water, casting a stark rippling shadow. "There it is." I steered starboard.

"Now we come about to port when we see the shark-tooth reef in front of us."

"Does it have three jagged teeth?"

"Yes."

"We're coming to it."

"Hard about." I forced the *Sea Cutter* into a sharp port turn.

Little by little we navigated our way through the reefs and wrecks.

"The last one looks like a Gorgon's head."

"It's to starboard."

I steered close to it, for just to starboard lay a wicked submerged reef.

The white cliffs rose high, waves roaring up their marble sides, while waterfalls poured out of dozens of caves and plummeted into the crashing sea.

"Find a place to hide."

I sailed along the cliffs until we came to a spot

where they parted as if they'd been cracked in half by a sledgehammer.

"Here."

I took the *Sea Cutter* far into the inlet where the sea calmed and dropped anchor, my hands quivering.

"I'm going to scout. Then we'll know the situation."

"Hurry," I begged.

"You don't hurry when you scout," Snake sneered.

He slipped over the gunwale, swimming to the cliffs. I watched him clambering up the moonlit face of the shiny marble, amazed at his dexterity. He went over the top and vanished.

Robo watched me dully, his pistol in his brace and his sword at his side.

"Can I see Wayland and Paulo now?" I chanced.

He said nothing, not a muscle on his face moving.

I stepped toward the companionway and he sprang to his feet, pulling his pistol.

"Why not?"

He merely motioned me away from the hatch with the pistol and then sat again, giving me the same blank look.

I could do nothing for my friends. My mind reverted to Father. I paced the deck, my stomach clenching. What if the Boar had killed him? I kept scanning the cliffs for Snake, but the moon set and dawn broke before I saw him climbing down the marble sides.

"What did you find?" I grabbed his arm as he hoisted himself over the gunwale.

"I found your father."

My stomach unclenched and warmth flooded through me.

"Please. When can I see him?"

He frowned. "It's exactly as I feared. The Boar and his crew hold your father and a dozen other shipwrecked sailors captive."

I paled. "How can we free him?"

"The pirates don't know we're here, so they're careless. Your father could get away if he knew where to meet you."

"Tonight?" I implored.

"Yes, tonight. Write him a note. Here, I have a paper and pen."

He unrolled an oiled pouch. From it he spread a piece of paper, handing me the pen and ink.

"What should I write?"

"Write this. 'Father, I've come for you. Meet me tonight at midnight by the split tree. Make sure you come alone.'"

"Why alone?"

"If he tries to help other captives escape with him, there's less chance he'll get away," he snapped.

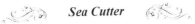

"Of course."

"Now sign it."

"Wait. I'll add something to show him it's really from me." I wrote, 'I played the game you told me to play,' and signed the letter.

"Excellent." He rolled the paper. "I'll sneak this note to him today. Then tonight—first my revenge, then your father."

"How can we catch the Boar alone?"

"Leave that to me. Now I'm off."

Snake wrapped the letter in oilskin and let himself off the *Sea Cutter*. Again I waited, pacing the deck, biting my lip 'til it bled. Suppose the Boar's crew captured Snake before he could deliver the note?

The sun set, the moon rose, and still no Snake. I grasped a shroud, trembling, staring at the cliffs. An eternity passed before I saw him scurrying down.

"It's done, but it took longer than I planned." He unrolled from an oilcloth the chronometer he'd stolen from Wayland. "Come on. We've got to hurry."

We swam to the base of the marble cliff. Up close, the stark white was veined with lines and swirls. Slippery, sharp ledges ran along the marble, most no more than an inch deep.

Handhold by handhold and step by step I struggled upward, trying to keep up with Snake's climb. My foot slipped, knocking my other foot off its ledge.

"Snake! Help!" I hung by my straining fingers high above the inlet. He grabbed my arm and helped me to the next ledge.

"Can't you even climb?" he growled.

When we got to the top, I collapsed, panting.

He pulled out Wayland's chronometer. "We don't have time to rest."

"What time is it?" I gasped.

"Ten. The Boar's already started out. Now hurry."

He led me across the cliff top to a dense forest, the long tree limbs twining around each other, and took a small path at a brisk stride.

I tried to match it, but the moon crosshatched the path, making it hard to tell the difference between the trees and their shadows. I tripped over a root, sprawling face first on the ground.

"You can't even walk," he snarled, yanking me to my feet. "If we don't finish the Boar fast, we won't be in time for your father."

I gripped the stitch in my side as we hastened down the path for what seemed to me at least two hours.

Snake put a hand on my shoulder. "Stop. This is the place."

"The time?" I wheezed.

He glanced at the chronometer. "We have an hour to

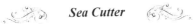

meet your father. You hide here in these bushes in the shadows. When the Boar comes, jump out and shout to distract him."

"What should I shout?"

"Let's see. Shout, 'This is Snake's revenge!' Now get in the bushes."

I ducked into the bushes, the branches scratching my cheeks. Snake climbed a tree limb above the path, behind where I'd stop the Boar.

He'd picked a poor place for my ambush, I thought. I'd be in moonlight when I jumped out on the path, but the Boar would be in the black shadows of big trees. I shivered, visualizing those tusks. What if the Boar didn't hesitate?

Footfalls crunched the path. I stopped breathing and crouched down further.

A tall form loomed in the shadows.

I jumped out in the moonlight. "This is Snake's revenge!" I yelled.

"Nat! What are you doing?" It was Father's voice.

Before I could get over my shock, Snake jumped from his limb onto Father's back.

"Your son is helping me kill you, Captain Childe," he chortled, plunging the dagger into his back.

"No!" I cried.

Father fell onto the moonlit path.

CHAPTER THIRTEEN
The Whirlpool

I ran toward Father, but armed men, strangely dressed, came crashing down the path. Two grabbed me while three others captured and disarmed Snake, although he cursed and struggled like a wild creature.

"Father!" I sobbed, horrified by the dark pool of blood spreading over his jacket.

One of the men put his ear to Father's mouth and then shook his head, speaking to the others in a strange tongue.

He couldn't be dead! I struggled to break free and dash to him, but the men held me tightly. More men rushed to us, and with them came Paulo. I was too anguished even to wonder how he got there.

"We were too late to stop the attack," a tall black man told Paulo.

"I'm so sorry, Nat," Paulo said. "The royal guards found us, and we told them what we had overheard when Snake made you write that note. We ran as fast as we could."

I hardly heard him. Everything seemed miles away.

"We must take these murderers to the king."

"But Nat isn't a murderer," Paulo protested.

"Yes, I am." I heard my father's voice again. *Nat! What are you doing?*

Three men lifted Father and ran with him, while the guards marched us in their wake. Snake thrashed about, but I stumbled along between my captors, my mind reeling.

Over and over, I saw Father fall headlong onto the path, saw the spreading pool of blood, saw the guard shake his head, until my mind numbed. My body staggered on.

* * *

My senses returned at dawn when we crested a hill overlooking a city made entirely of white marble. In the center stood a palace covered with seashells and stained-glass windows, the place where the king would judge me. Good. I wanted to be condemned.

We marched to the palace, where men on each side

of massive double doors lifted conch shells to their lips and blew a smooth note. The doors swung open.

Murals of the ocean adorned the hall, and a line of heralds, some white, some black, stood on each side, raising their conch shells and blowing a commanding blast as we passed.

At the end of the room sat an old but regal black man with a thin circlet of gold on his grizzled head. His robes shone with embroidered gold thread and he held a staff topped with a giant pearl. Wayland stood beside him.

"Wayland…" I started, but I could say no more.

"I understand, Nat," he answered, sympathy in his eyes.

"Are you Nathaniel Childe, the son of our beloved governor?" the king asked. "He has spoken many times of you. I had hoped to meet you in different circumstances, but now I must be here to judge you. The ancient books of the law, handed down to my father from his, and from his father before him, decree it." He stamped his staff on the floor. "The law proclaims the punishment for attacking a man—the whirlpool of death."

Wayland started, his eyes flashing.

I nodded, for I wanted to die as soon as I could.

"Now wait just a minute. You don't think the son of

the governor would kill his own father, do you?" Snake demanded. "We heard other people attacking his father and rushed in to help him—but we were too late. Isn't that right, Nat?"

He hissed so only I could hear, "If you die, your mother will grow old with no one to help her." He sickened me, for this must've been the line he planned to use to get me to help him off the island after he'd killed Father.

"You must be Snake," the king said, a note like cold steel in his voice. "What do you say, Nathaniel? Is Snake's story true? Shall I let you both go?"

"He lies! We killed Father."

Snake broke away from his captors, sidestepping the guards who sprang at him.

"Close the doors!" the king commanded.

The huge doors swung toward each other, but Snake slipped between them before they slammed.

Wayland raced toward a shadow fleeing past a stained-glass window that depicted the sun. He dove right through the sun, shattering the glass and catching Snake around the ankles.

Snake screamed and writhed as he fell, but Wayland pinned his arms behind his back and thrust him, still struggling, back into the hall.

"You will not like what you are about to see," the

king said to Snake.

From a doorway behind the king two guards entered, carrying a chair that they set down to the right-hand side of the king. A man sat, hunched over, with bandages wound around the middle of his body. He raised his head.

"Father!"

Snake wailed.

At a nod from the king, the guards released me and I ran to Father, throwing myself on my knees, wrapping my arms around his legs.

"Father," I wept.

He cradled my head in his lap. "My poor son," he kept muttering.

He looked up at the king. "I don't feel right sitting in your presence, my lord."

"I am glad to have you at my right hand, sitting or standing."

"But, my lord, this is a court of judgment today, and I'm here to plead for the life of my son."

"You have served as my governor for four years, Jonathan. You know the book of the law better than anyone but me. The law is clear. We must throw Snake and your son into the whirlpool of death."

"But there is another law, my lord. An older law. It says that a father may take the place of his son for any punishment. I choose to be thrown into the whirlpool instead of Nathaniel."

The king nodded. "It is what I thought you would do, my friend."

"Wait. No. You can't do that," I protested. "I don't agree to it! You go back to Mother."

"Whether you agree to it or not makes no difference," said the king. "It is your father's choice."

"But he's right," Wayland said with an odd smile. "Jonathan can't die for Nat."

"Wayland! You stay out of this!" Father demanded.

"No. I will not, Jonathan." He turned to the king. "My lord, Jonathan can't die in Nat's place, because I'm Nat's true father."

My life turned a somersault.

Wayland crouched beside me, rubbing my back.

"My wife, your mother, died when you were born, Nat. Who would take care of you while I was at sea? My closest friends had been praying for a child for years and years. I gave you to them, Nat, but I never stopped loving you."

"You're my father?" Still stunned, I stared at his kindly face.

"You must still always think of Jenny and Jon as your parents."

"But you're still my best friend. I can't let you die."

"Is what Wayland has said true?" the king asked Father.

"It is. But I raised Nathaniel. It is I who should die for him."

"The law says nothing about who raised the child. It is a question of blood. If Wayland is Nathaniel's blood father, then only he can be the sacrifice."

"No…!" Father started, but he slumped down in a swoon from too much effort after his injury.

"The law says there is to be no delay." The king stood, pounding his staff. "Guards, carry my governor back to his bedchamber. Take Wayland and Snake to the whirlpool of death."

"Where is this whirlpool?" I cried, facing the king with my fists clenched. "I'll throw myself into it before I let you throw Wayland in."

"That shall not be," said the king. He signaled and a guard grabbed me.

"But it's my fault," I pleaded.

"Nat, I gave you to your parents once, and the family that grew around you was the most wonderful thing I've ever known," Wayland said. "Now make me happy by letting me give them to you a second time."

"I don't want you to die!"

"Only my body will die." He put his hand on my shoulder. "I shall go to be with my Lord."

The guards forced Wayland and Snake toward the door, Snake writhing and twisting. "You can't kill me! I can't die!" he screamed, frothing at the mouth. "No! I'll get away and kill you. Do you hear me? I'll kill you!" Then his voice dropped into a wheedling whine. "But if you let me go now I swear I'll go away and never come back. I swear it."

The king ignored Snake and commanded the doors thrown open. A noisy crowd had formed outside, but the people quieted as soon as they saw the prisoners.

The king stood at the top of the steps while his heralds blew sharply on their conch shells. He spoke in his own language, pointing at the thrashing Snake, and angry shouts rippled through the crowd.

He raised his hand, saying something while indicating Wayland, and the crowd quieted to respectful murmurs, some coming over to touch Wayland.

The king gave a command, pounding the marble step, and the people parted as our group marched through, then closed behind us and followed.

The guard gripped my arm tightly, but I relaxed it, making no attempt to struggle, for I had a plan.

Before I saw the whirlpool I heard it, churning like angry surf beating on the shore. As we drew closer, the roar shook the air and trembled the ground. We rounded a bend and I saw a pool that whirled madly, like water racing down a drain.

The whirlpool had ripped boulders out of the cliff on its far shore, and these hunkered half in the water with the current surging around and over them in wild torrents. A deceptive calm spot waited at the center, where the pool sucked a person straight down.

The king led us to the edge and lifted his staff.

I tore from my guard's relaxed grasp and charged toward the pool. If I were already dead, there'd be no reason for Wayland to act as my substitute.

The king leaped over and grabbed my shoulder with a grip like iron.

"You shall stay with me."

"No!" I shouted, struggling in vain.

He raised his staff again and addressed Snake and Wayland. Snake's eyes were rolling up in his head and he was talking to himself, froth dripping from his chin.

"You are here to be thrown into the whirlpool of death to pay for the murderous attack on our beloved governor," the king said. "Once you are thrown into the waters of the whirlpool, the crime is paid for."

He looked directly at Wayland. "You, my friend, go into the water as a substitute for the governor's son. It is a noble action. May much happiness and love grow out of it."

He stepped closer to Wayland and spoke to him in a low voice. "My friend, no one can swim against the current. No one can help being sucked down. I advise you not to struggle. Do you understand?"

He looked right into Wayland's eyes. Wayland nodded.

"Throw in the prisoners!" the king commanded.

It happened so fast, I wasn't prepared, and perhaps that's what the king wanted.

The guards flung both men into the pool, where the current caught them. Snake immediately struck out swimming frantically, trying to get back to shore.

"Swim!" I yelled to Wayland.

He looked at me and shook his head.

Snake got nowhere, still pinned beside Wayland by the savage torrent. The pool swirled both men toward the center, Wayland gently treading water while Snake redoubled his swimming, alternately screaming at us for help and cursing at us, spluttering water.

Someone laid a sympathetic hand on my back. Paulo stood next to me, profound sadness in his eyes as he watched Wayland and Snake be swept right to the deadly calm center of the pool.

Wayland searched the shore until he found me and lifted his hand in farewell.

My mind jumped back to when he had pressed his

forehead against mine. "You've just shown me you're a real sailor, Nat," he had said. "But even if you weren't, you'd still be my favorite boy."

"My favorite man," I mumbled, my voice trembling.

Snake stopped swimming and grabbed Wayland, clawing at him, trying to lift himself clear of the water, then wrapping his arms around Wayland and screaming in stark horror. The center caught and whirled them around so fast they seemed to blend together.

They both disappeared. The pool was empty. Empty.

Snake broke the surface with the most terrified shriek I'd ever heard. He thrashed the water for less than a second and was sucked down again.

Wayland never came up at all.

CHAPTER FOURTEEN
The Stream

The king lifted his hand from my shoulder and stretched out his arm.

"You are free."

"I hate you!" I spat back, and ran away into the surrounding forest—away from the king, away from the whirlpool, away from the crowd, away from Paulo and Father.

I could never, ever forgive myself. I hated myself.

I dashed through the forest, the tree branches filtering shafts of sunlight that blurred with my tears. My stomach ached, not with hunger, but with a deeper emptiness. When I couldn't run any more, I stumbled on over ridges and across valleys until I had no idea how to get back. Far enough.

I leaned against a mossy tree bent over a bubbling stream. My parched mouth longed for the water, but I ignored it. I wanted to die, and I could die of thirst faster than I could die of hunger.

A fire had hollowed the moss-covered tree. I curled inside it, wrapping my hands around my knees.

The sun set, but that meant nothing to me except that the sun was dying, like everything died. The stars came out between the branches of the forest. They had once held a promise for me, but now they looked like cold worlds that didn't care what happened on Earth. They ignored Wayland's death, while I cried myself to sleep.

A desert filled my mouth when I woke, but I refused to leave my cave and drink. It grew worse the next day, and I drifted in and out of consciousness.

I woke to sunlight. Wayland stood before me, smiling.

"Wayland!"

"Nat, have you ever looked closely at my face?"

"Lots of times."

"No. Really looked. You thought the lines on my face shaped my smile. Look again. Remember, I gave you to your parents because my wife died."

I studied his face and saw that a sorrow and grief too

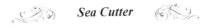

deep to be named had etched the wrinkles, but the four strong laugh lines at the corners of his eyes turned them into part of his smile.

"I taught myself to laugh again," he said. "I'll never cease missing my wife, but there can be joy after grief, I promise you."

"What should I do to be like you?"

"Drink of the fresh stream. It may be fed by tears, but you can also hear it laughing. Follow it."

I woke truly. A dream. Wayland was gone, but his message of hope remained. I stretched numb, deadened hands to my cave's wall, trying to pull myself up, but I fell. I couldn't even crawl, so I wriggled out of the cave, my returning senses stinging like sharp needles.

As dawn broke, I squirmed to the stream and dunked my head in. The cold, delicious drink flowed into my body, strengthening me, bringing me life.

I rose and followed the stream. Where it flowed around rocks, ripples spread to bounce against ripples, making a checkerboard of sparkling light. Here and there, narrow rocky banks and twisting drops tortured the stream into surging, falling cataracts that seemed to roar in fierce, angry determination to burst through.

In one place, an odd elbow of the stream formed a deep, quiet pool. A large old fish ruled over the hidden depths, and I pictured him as an ancient king thinking lonely thoughts, while just beside the pool the water laughed as it tumbled over a ledge.

Other streams joined mine, turning it into a calm, deep river. The sky turned from robin's-egg blue to the royal blue of evening before the forest thinned. Ahead I saw mown grass and flowers. I staggered onto the lawn.

"Nat!" Paulo ran and threw his arms around me.

"Nathaniel!" Father cried out from his chair. "Come here, my son!"

Paulo slipped an envelope into my hand—Mother's letter to me.

"I found this on the *Sea Cutter*."

I stumbled to Father, who reached out for me. I buried my head in his hug, smelling the special warmth that meant Father. My body, and my whole being, rested—until I remembered the letter and broke the embrace.

"Father, I have something I must show you." I handed him the letter.

"From Mother to you! She is well? Oh, how I miss her!"

He read the letter and gave it back.

"I'm glad you got Mother's permission, Nathaniel. You did the right thing."

"Got her permission?"

I looked at the letter. The first line read: "Dear Nat, On no account do you have my approval to sail to Perlas Grandes...." But the second line read: "... without Wayland! You do have my permission to sail with him on the Sea Cutter to search for Father...."

I closed the letter with which Snake had tricked me.

"I didn't think I had permission. I lied to Wayland, and now he's dead. I miss him, Father. He—" I couldn't go on.

"I miss him too." He stroked my hair. "Why don't you tell me everything?"

The whole story tumbled out. "So it's my fault Wayland's dead," I ended.

"Snake bears the most blame," he said.

"If I hadn't lied to Wayland, none of this would've happened."

He took my chin and raised my eyes to his. "Then thank goodness for forgiveness."

* * *

Paulo and I found Perlas Grandes a wondrous island. When I wasn't walking through the woods by myself thinking about Wayland, Paulo and I spent hours hiking wide ledges on the white cliffs, even exploring some of the caves from which streams plummeted into the sea far below.

We drew pictures of the strange furry creatures that

scuttled along the branches with human-looking little hands and rings around their tails. We played hide-and-go-seek in the palace. The king even let me hide behind his throne once. Paulo didn't find me.

We spent much of the time diving through water as clear as sky. Coral reefs sang along the bottom of the sea floor with melodies of oranges, yellows, reds, and greens. What looked like red plants jerked closed if we touched them. Funny spotted crabs ran in and out of the niches of the coral, rearing at us with their eyes bulging and their claws up like they were challenging us to a fistfight.

Schools of small darting yellow fish flashed like gold clouds. If we dove right through them, they parted around us in a golden shimmer that was like diving into the sun. Flat fish dressed boldly with broad, iridescent yellow and blue stripes drifted lazily around the reef, nibbling at larvae. Large silver fish streaked down and gobbled them while they were still eating their own supper.

I wished I understood each of the animals and plants. I sketched them from memory, noticing that some were more alike than others. I organized my sketches into piles, trying to put similar animals and plants into the same pile.

Yet, in the middle of these pleasures, Wayland's

absence often hit me in the stomach, and I'd go off to cry. Even when exploring with Paulo, I found myself turning to point something out to Wayland—only to find him gone.

Paulo and I worked together to find pearls. We'd pick the largest oyster—so big we had to bring it up together—then pry it open. As the shell parted, we held our breath, and on our fourth day we found a magnificent pearl. We gave it to the king because all pearls on the island belonged to him.

That's why, when they found it, they gave the king the pearl Snake had stolen.

"Why did Snake hate you?" I asked Father.

"For turning him over to the law."

"What for?"

"One winter, right after I got the pearl, I caught him trying to break into my steel chest in my lodgings."

"You weren't at sea?"

"I had business on land while Wayland minded the *Christopher*. Snake and I fought with swords until I knocked his from his hands, pinning him to the wall with my point."

"I can imagine his expression."

"It got worse when the law came to hang him. He swore he'd escape and get revenge, but I sailed away without giving it a second thought."

"So Wayland never saw him?"

"Never even heard of him. I thought Snake was dangling on the noose."

"But he wasn't."

Father nodded. "That's how it began."

* * *

Three weeks passed before Father recovered enough to sail. The king held a ceremony of leave-taking as everyone came down to see us off. They weren't seafarers themselves, for the wood of their trees warped and split when cured—no good for boats.

Only two of the shipwrecked men wished to return with us to the colonies. Herman Stevenson had a wife in Provincetown, and Robert Melville hoped he still had a sweetheart in Boston.

Robo was given a choice—go back with us and face the gallows or stay on the island as the king's servant. He mustn't have been as stupid as he looked, for he chose to stay.

The king directed his farewell to Father. I wish I knew everything he said, but Father understood the language and kept shaking his blushing head as the king made declarations to which the people applauded.

Then, to my surprise, the king called to me and held out the dagger. "A master forger crafted this long ago, forming a word on the hilt, young governor's son."

I hadn't noticed the word before, because it was in
the island's alphabet and intermingled with decoration.

"I don't know what that word is, my lord."

"'Truth.' I am giving this dagger back to you,
Nathaniel Childe. You lost it before by not telling the
truth. Do you understand?"

I flushed hot. "I understand."

The king's expression softened, and he dismissed me
with a kind nod, turning again to Father. He pulled
from his robes a pearl almost as large as the one on his
staff. The crowd murmured.

"I found this pearl when I was your son's age. I give
it to you."

Father looked from the pearl to the king.

"Thank you, my lord."

"Sail now," said the king, a bit brusquely. "But I
have one last command."

"Yes, my lord?"

"Sail past the white cliffs before you head to the open
sea. Now go."

Father still wasn't fit enough to help with the sailing,
but we had four able-bodied seamen who put the *Sea
Cutter* underway. A lump formed in my throat as we
pulled away from the island on which Wayland had
died.

"Why does the king want us to sail past the white

cliffs?" I asked Father, as they loomed into view.

"I don't know."

We sailed, searching the cliffs, until I spotted something high on a ledge by a waterfall. It looked like…. Could it really be? No. Surely it couldn't. But it was. I was sure of it.

"There's Wayland!" I cried.

We all jumped to our feet, Wayland already waving at us. He stretched out his arms, studied the sea, and dove. Perfect timing. An outgoing wave swept him away from the cliffs, and we shortly had him in the boat, all of us laughing for joy.

"How did you survive the whirlpool?" I gasped.

"The king told me not to struggle. It struck me that the whirlpool had to drain somewhere, so I decided to use all my strength to swim down in the same direction as the current. I came out in a cave and followed it to the ledge. I've been living on bird's eggs."

"The king knew," said Father. "He sent us to find you."

"I wish he would've sent you a little sooner," Wayland laughed.

Father looked back toward the island. "Even I have never fully understood the king."

CHAPTER FIFTEEN
New Bedford

We left Herman Stevenson with his overjoyed wife in Provincetown, and Robert Melville in Boston, where his sweetheart had waited for six years.

As the sun set, we spotted the towering masts of the New Bedford harbor. An ember glowed in my chest, for Mother and Father would see each other again at last.

I was too distracted to notice that Paulo seemed pensive, but Father noticed.

"What's wrong, Paulo? Do you regret choosing not to go back to Brazil?"

"No. I'm glad to be starting a new life here, but it's a little scary. I knew how to take care of myself in

Recife, but will I know how to in New Bedford?"

"Take care of yourself!" Father shook his head. "There's been a terrible misunderstanding. We're not sailing you here to abandon you, but to live with us."

Paulo grinned shyly. "Do you really mean it?"

Father laughed, his hand on Paulo's shoulder. "But you might not want to come live with us, because I'm afraid then I would insist you become Nat's brother, and we all know what he's like."

"I've always wanted a brother," Paulo said, grinning even wider.

"Hooray!" I cheered.

* * *

We bound the *Sea Cutter* to her slip, but my hands were shaking so hard I couldn't help de-rig her. I dropped blocks and tangled lines. Seeing my state, Wayland told my father we three should go while he finished.

I went over to him, wanting to say something before we parted, but I didn't know what.

He saw the look in my eyes and pulled me into an embrace. I answered his hug, wrapping my arms tightly around him.

"I know," he murmured. "I feel the same way. How could I not, after all we've been through together? Now go. Go to your mother."

When we reached town, the dark streets were almost empty. Fragrant suppers cooked over musky-smelling wood fires while lanterns glowed through curtained windows.

As we strode toward our home, the quietness of the town fell over us, each of us intent on what lay a few moments ahead. Paulo would meet his new mother, and Father would see Mother for the first time in four years. I would get to see the look on Mother's face.

A warm, golden radiance shone behind the curtains of our home, smoke drifting out of the chimney. Our footsteps on the cobblestones echoed off the walls as we reached our stout, red door. Father raised his hand to knock, but hesitated. He looked at me.

"Thank you, Nathaniel," he said. "Thank you for coming to get me."

Then he knocked. A graceful, light step sounded inside the house and Mother opened the door.

THE END

Look for
Red Stone
Book II
The Chronicles of Nathaniel Childe